Randal H. Roberts

The Silver Trout

And other stories

Randal H. Roberts

The Silver Trout
And other stories

ISBN/EAN: 9783744750639

Printed in Europe, USA, Canada, Australia, Japan

Cover: Foto ©Andreas Hilbeck / pixelio.de

More available books at **www.hansebooks.com**

THE SILVER TROUT

AND

OTHER STORIES.

BY

SIR RANDAL H. ROBERTS, BART.

("LIGHT CAST"),

OF *LAND AND WATER* AND LATE OF THE *FIELD,*

AUTHOR OF "MODERN WAR," "THE RIVER'S SIDE,' "GLENMÁHRA,"
IN THE SHIRES," ETC. ETC.

LONDON:
W. H. ALLEN & CO., 13 WATERLOO PLACE,
PALL MALL. S.W.

1888.

PREFACE.

———◆———

Most of the stories contained in this little volume
have from time to time appeared in the columns of
the *Field* and *Land and Water*.

I have thought publication in book form might,
perhaps, serve to pass away a weary hour, and afford
the sportsman some amusement, as treating of his
favourite pursuits.

If I have in any way had the good fortune to
accomplish my object, or to contribute one moment's
pleasure to my brethren of the gun or rod, I shall
feel amply repaid for any trouble these few pages
have cost me.

R. H. ROBERTS.

London, April 5th, 1887.

CONTENTS.

THE SILVER TROUT.

A Legend of the River's Side.

———◆———

IT was the height of the London season. The sun glared down into the streets from a clear blue sky, with never a cloud to shelter one from its burning rays. I sat in my studio lazily repainting the foreground of a bit of Dartmoor scenery, cursing the fate that kept me, a poor artist, in town whilst I ought to have been making studies from Nature in the country, when my door was unceremoniously thrown open, and an old Oxford chum burst in.

" Hullo, old man! what's the matter? why didn't you answer my letter? "

" For the very best of reasons," I replied, " I never got it."

" Confound that servant of mine. I daresay he has it in his pocket now. However, there's lots of time.

Come, pack up your things, get your fishing tackle and painting things and come with me for a week. I've arranged everything. Got anything to drink? This is awfully thirsty weather."

"My dear friend, it is impossible. In the first place, I can't afford it, and——"

"Oh, bosh! who asked *you* to afford it; and since when is it that such formality has sprung up between Charles Haughton and Jack Leslie? Where the dickens do you keep that drink?"

"My dear Jack, you'll find it in that cupboard; but, as to your offer, I must really decline."

"Decline be hanged," he cried, opening a bottle of soda-water; "come, old man, you can pay me back when that picture's sold. By the way, how much do you want for it? Never mind answering now, but hurry up, and whilst you're packing I'll tell you where we are going."

It was no use, for when Jack Leslie made up his mind there was no resisting him, and, as the sequel proved, this little holiday had very nearly a very serious effect upon my future life.

"Have you ever been down to ——shire?" asked Jack, whilst standing with his back to an imaginary fire in an empty grate, with his coat-tails under his arms.

"Never," I replied.

"Well, then, you'll enjoy yourself. I'm going down to stop at a farmhouse with the jolliest old couple you ever knew. They've only one bedroom, but there are two beds in it. I've sent down some liquor and some other little comforts; for the rest, we must depend upon the fowl-yard and the dairy; and last, but not least, I've got three and a half miles of the loveliest trout-stream within a hundred miles of London. Now, old man, which prospect suits you best—this stifling studio or my farmhouse in ——shire, eh?"

" My dear Jack, your description settles me at once, if I really ever had any hesitation."

" By the way, there's a lovely old mill down there that ought to pay you for the whole trip."

All I had to do was to overhaul my tackle, and whilst doing this I was debating in my mind what the odds were in favour of fishing against painting; and I am free to confess that the chances of the former predominated. All this time Jack Leslie was looking over a portfolio of sketches and sipping his brandy and soda.

" I'll tell you what it is, Charley, if you won't mind my saying so, there's a want of life in your studies. Why don't you stick in a girl wearing a red petticoat and a blue bodice, every now and then, or something like that? This is a jolly sketch (holding it up); ' A cast up stream.' The man's capital."

" Well, old man, you're right, and I'm going to make some studies of rustics, &c., on this occasion." Little did I know what this would lead to at the time.

A smart-going Hansom soon landed us at the station, where a first-class carriage was quickly piled with our impedimenta, and in a couple of hours' time, after having been whirled through that most lovely scenery which the home counties alone can afford, we arrived at our destination.

Standing on the platform, rigged out in his Sunday clothes, stood our host, as fine a specimen of the British yeoman as one would wish to see.

"How be you, Muster Leslie," he commenced, giving Jack a hearty shake of the hand; "and you, Sir, you be the painter, I suppose. You're welcome, Sir"; and, without waiting for a reply, and anticipating Jack's question, he continued: "The trout be a rising that mad, Muster Leslie, you can scarce see the water for 'em. You knows I b'aint much of a fisherman; but says I to my old woman, says I, 'Muster Leslie will have rare sport.' But coom on, Sir, cart's a waitin', and maybe you'll like a seat."

"No, thank you, Joshua, my friend and I will walk. It's only a couple of miles," he added, turning to me, "and part of the road runs by the river-side, going by the old mill. There's no such thing as a fly down here, old man, so you must walk unless you like to be jolted to pieces in that cart." We soon struck the river. What a sight to gladden the heart of any angler, much more an unfortunate, worn-out artist. Fringed here and there with rows of willows, whilst an occasional old pollard stretched its gnarled trunk across the water, creating darksome shadows, a swift-running stream, from fifty to one hundred feet in width, flowed smoothly between and over long banks of swaying weeds; sometimes over a gravelly bed, creating a gentle stickle; anon gliding over an alluvial bottom; now losing itself in a sharp bend, making a deep but clear eddy on the one side and a still pool on the other, and finally, after a tortuous course, each nook and bend of which promised a harbour for big fish, the rapidity of the stream was lost in the waters of an old mill-dam. Here and there, too, on either bank grew a sturdy oak or a thorn-bush, whilst a paling ran out into the stream, each post making a refuge for a fish behind it.

And then the mill, how shall I describe it? There are mills and mills; but the only mill the fisherman loves to think of is that one the very sight of which tells him intuitively that, round and about it, in the mill-head and in the mill-tail, the heavy fish do congregate. Yes! the dear old wooden mill, with its red-tiled roof, toned down with moss and lichen, the small quaint windows, the open door just above the sluice, looking up the river; the whole building painted white, except where the projecting angles are covered with the equally white flour-dust: the hum of the grindstone, as it is impelled by the old wheel, and the miller's boy, lazily smoking his pipe and leaning across the footbridge watching the swallows as they skim across the mill-pool, whilst an occasional circle here and there tells one that the trout are feeding. Dear reader, can you see the picture? I shall never forget it, for it is here that I encountered much which had a most profound influence upon my future life. Do you believe in the supernatural? Do you believe in Fate?—in Kismet? If so, listen, for I am about to tell you a story, which you can believe or not, as you like—a story of love and a ghost fish.

I shall not pause to describe the farmhouse where we stayed, or its surroundings. There are hundreds of them to be seen, with all their wealth of comfort and solidity, in the home counties. Four walls and a roof on top, four windows, a green door and a brass knocker, with a gravel path up to that said green door, pretty well covers the architectural and other descriptions. Suffice it to say that comfort and plenty reigned supreme, and that for cleanliness and civility, Mr. and Mrs. Joshua Whitcomb ought to take the palm in any community.

We soon settled down, Jack and I, in our comfortable bedroom, unpacked our traps, taking, of course, our fishing paraphernalia down with us to the common sitting-room, where a cozy table spread out for the evening meal awaited us. After supper Jack and I naturally fell to the task of sorting our tackle, which soon covered the table, whilst old Joshua, seated in an arm-chair, lit his pipe and joined us in a glass of grog.

"Well, Joshua," said Jack, extricating a mass of flies and casting-lines from a tin box, "and how is Mr. Tomlin, the miller?"

"Well, Sir," replied Joshua, sipping his grog, "he be main the same as ever, only a bit more cantankerous about that there mill-head. You know the old story, and it do seem as he grows older as if he believed more in it."

"Oh! to be sure; the queer story, or absurd nonsense, I ought to say, about the silver trout. You don't mean to say he still keeps to that?"

"Indeed, but he do, Sir, and more serious nor ever."

"The silver trout," said I. "What on earth does that mean?"

"Oh!" replied Jack, "that is a mystery which forms part and parcel of the attraction which I intended you to enjoy during your stay down here. Well, old man, it's almost a ghost story—at least, a fishy one."

"That it be, Muster Leslie; my old woman and I don't lay much store by such fal-lals, yet it do seem kinder strange and onnatural."

"What's the mystery?" said I, beginning to feel interested.

"Well," replied Jack, "I'm not quite well up in it,

but Joshua here knows all about it, as, indeed, does the whole country-side, for the matter of that; so Joshua, while I get this blessed tangle out, freshen your glass, and tell Mr. Haughton the tale."

Thus requested, Joshua refilled his glass, settled himself in his arm-chair, and told us the following strange story.

"Well, gentlemen, you must know that old Bill Tomlin—I say old, for he must be nigh on to three-score and ten—and his father before him, have owned the mill, and the meadow above the mill-head, for many years. When old Bill was nigh on to forty-five he married, and the folks they stared, because Bill had always been a wild kind of a chap, and not sich an one as would make a good husband. Well, gentlemen, one day, just after haymaking, Bill went up to London, and when he come back he brought a wife back wi' 'im. The neighbours and country folk round about warn't much pleased. They said there was lots of nice girls about, and what did he want to go and bring a stranger down to the old mill. Still they was all main anxious to see her, out of curiosity like, and Bill he was only too glad to let 'em do so; and well he might, for a prettier, modester, kind-hearteder, Christianer young woman I never set my eyes on than Mrs. William Tomlin. Lord bless yer! Muster Leslie, if this gentleman had seen her he ud 'ave made his fortun a paintin' her. When I see'd her first, says my old

woman to me, 'she's kind o' delicate, Jos'; but I
laughed, and said that ——shire air would soon bring the
roses to her cheeks; and so it did, and Bill he drove a
roaring trade, and all the country round come to see
his beautiful wife, and things went well wi' 'em. Well,
gentlemen, in time, the Lord, in His goodness, give him
three children; but, alack! Sirs, they was all girls,
and never a boy came, to hand the old mill over to; and
when the third little one was born—that's Dora that
is now, Muster Leslie—as you know, poor old Bill lost
his wife. Well, gentlemen, from that day it seems as
if nothing but misfortune come to Bill Tomlin—not
as his business got bad, but somehow he seemed to
change. First, he wouldn't grind everybody's corn;
then he wouldn't let anybody fish in the mill-head or
the meadow; and one day, when he caught the curate
a fishing there, he threw him right into the river, and
never went to church arter. Why, I don't know, for
the curate was main sorry. Well, the daughters they
grew up, and, as time went on, they bloomed and
blossomed into beautiful flowers, like their poor
mother, and full of that sweetness and gentleness that
had made her loved by everyone. You'll excuse me,
gentlemen," said old Joshua, wiping his eyes with his
coat-sleeve, and taking a strong swallow from his glass,
" but I get kinder foolish when I think of her and her
little ones, as is all gone 'cept Miss Dora as is, bless
her heart!"

"All gone?" said I, interrupting him, for I was now fairly interested.

"Yes, Sir, I'll tell you all about it. It's a queer tale; and while I think of it, Muster Leslie, don't fish the mill-head to-morrow. I know old Bill wouldn't like to deny you; but he's been very cranky the last few weeks, and maybe you would excuse him."

"All right, Joshua, go ahead with the yarn. You tell it better every time I hear you."

"Thank you kindly, Sir. Well the girls grew up, and about three years ago the old Squire he died up at the Manor House, and the place, with the shooting and sporting, was let to an officer, who come down and took possession. Well, somehow he made acquaintance with old Bill, who was always a bit of a sportsman, you know, and he commenced to talk to Bill about improving the river, and said as how he wanted to put some new trout in. Bill didn't like this, as he was always very conservative; but somehow the Captain he got round him, and some beautiful fresh trout was turned in just above the bend of the old mill-head. I wish them trouts had been all boiled before they was put in. I wish—well, excuse me, gentlemen, I'm d——d if I do know what I *do* wish," said the old man, striking the table heavily with his hand; "but, mind you, I don't believe it. I goes to church regular, and I tell you I don't believe it. About this time Bill was took ill of a fever, and while he had that fever there came upon him a feeling that those trout as was turned in was a going to work mischief. One night he got out of his bed when no one was watching, and got an old net down as he kept for keeping the jack out of the water, and he tried to drag the mill-head above, and was found nigh dead on the bank. I must tell you, gents, that some of these trout had been caught, and they were quite white and silvery, not like our own trout down here, but quite different. The Captain he said it was because they were not used to the change. Howsomdever, while Bill lay ill, Clara, his eldest daughter, she went off, and has never been heer'd on since. The Captain went away at the same time, and he give up the Manor House too. Then a painter gentleman come down—excuse me, Sir," said the old man, looking at me—"no disrespect; he took the Manor House, and he come down, and he painted the old mill, and old Bill, and the old mastiff, and my missus, and the parson, and the church, and most everything round; and Bill Tomlin, who had just got over his illness, and was sore tried about Clara, he seemed to take to the painter gentleman. Well, the painter was main fond of fishing, and somehow he found that the mill-head and tail, and the meadow above was the best ground, especially when Miss Mary—that was the second daughter—was about. Since Bill Tomlin's illness, the neighbours said he was queer in his head. I never saw it. Only he made hard bargains about grinding the

corn, and put up ever so many posts warning people
from fishing. But one day he come down to me, and
I got a bit scared. Says he to me, ' Josh, do you know
there's a silver trout in the mill-head, and if I don't
catch him, I shall lose Mary. She and the silver trout
is a going somehow. They're going through the wheel
into the race, and then the corn will be ground blood
red.' I tried to soften him down ; but no, I must come,
he said, that night, and help him with the net. Of
course, I promised him, never intending, and I saw
him back to the mill, and I told Miss Mary I thought
her father was kinder strange ; but the painter gentleman was there, and she seemed only to heed him. Next
morning Miss Mary was gone and the painter too, and
old Bill lay on his bed near to his death, talking nothing
but about a silver trout in the mill-head. That is two
year ago, gentlemen, and Bill is better, although he
ain't heard of Clara or Mary. Dora, as you know, is
at home, Muster Leslie ; but what is queer is that there
is a silver trout left in the mill-head, and that old Bill
won't let anyone fish there for fear of catching it."

"Why not ? " I asked, deeply interested.

" Because, Sir, Bill says when that trout is caught
he'll lose his life and his only daughter."

" What bosh ! " exclaimed Jack ; " here, let's have
another drain and to bed ; I'll bet we'll catch this same
silver trout." Upon which old Joshua rose, and, in a
most sepulchral voice, and with deep meaning, said :—

"For the love of heaven, gentlemen, don't, don't try. The silver trout is not a fish; it is the spirit of poor Mrs. Tomlin as has gone into a trout, so as to be near all she loved, and I'm sure of it."

Old Joshua's story haunted me all night. I could not sleep, and was up with the sun in the morning. As I threw open the window and leaned out, the scene reminded me of a similar one, which an Irishman—a natural poet—whom I met in the west of Ireland, thus quaintly described :

> One morning bright and glorious,
> When the wild birds sang a chorious,
> And all nature was uprorious,
> In the charming month of May,
> When the lambs and trouts and horses,
> That know not what remorse is,
> And the salmon, whale and porpoise
> They gambolled in the sea.

Jack Leslie was snoring hard, and I had not the heart to wake him; but back to bed I could not go. That prophetic warning of old Joshua's seemed to jangle in my ears—"Don't fish for the silver trout," and yet the very fact of being told not to do so made me more anxious to find out something about this strange old miller and his daughter.

The mill wasn't far off. How would it be to walk down there and be back in time for breakfast? I might make a sketch, and I might—well, I didn't exactly know what might happen.

I was soon dressed and on my way to the mill. It was, I should say, about five o'clock, and a lovely morning. There was not a breath of wind, and the day augured badly for fishing. However, " Many a bright, sunshiny morning turns out a dark and cloudy day," says the old fishing song, and so I hoped it would. A short half hour's walk brought me to the mill. I walked up on to the bank at the mill-head, which was like a sheet of glass, except where, here and there, the gentle suck of a trout made a tiny ring upon the still surface. Well, here was the spot of last night's curious story, and here must be the "silver trout," without the shadow of a doubt. I looked with curiosity at the water, reflecting the while as to the exact spot whereabouts that fish might lie. Just then a short cough caused me to look up, and I saw an old man, very much bent, and leaning on a stick, standing on the opposite bank, carrying a basket in his hands. He evidently had not observed me, so, taking it for granted that this must be the miller, I hid behind an alder-bush and watched him. First of all the old man knelt down upon the bank, and commenced muttering, all the while keeping his gaze fixed upon the water. Then he took something out of the basket, which he threw into the water. A commotion and a splashing ensued, and I could plainly see the tail of a large trout as it broke the surface.

"The Silver Trout!" I mentally exclaimed, and a rare big fish, too. My angler's spirit was in arms. I vowed not only to catch that fish, but also to solve the whole mystery. Whilst thinking over how this was to be done, I heard one of the sweetest of voices calling from the mill, " Father ! father ! why didn't you wait for me ? " and immediately afterwards there came tripping on the scene a girl that you see only once in a lifetime ; at least, I think so.

" Well, how 's the dear old trout to-day ? " she asked ; " and are you——" Just then she caught sight of me behind the alder-bush. " Father, there 's someone on the other side of the stream." The old man looked up, and, shading his eyes with his hand, said :

" So there be, girl. Coom away; don't ee stand glaring there. Coom away, Dora, I say. I dreamed about it, girl, I did, and I saw them both and the silver trout. Coom away ; the Captain will excuse us."

" That 's not the Captain, father."

" Oh, yes it be ; he told me last night he was coming to fish, and bring—— well, no matter."

" Come, father, breakfast will be ready; let us go in."

" Aye, aye, the Captain ; he 'll not be long, he 'll not be long " ; and, muttering to himself, he disappeared through the door into the mill with the young girl, who, I naturally concluded from what I had heard, was Dora, his youngest daughter.

It was now getting on to eight o'clock, and the appearance of the weather had entirely altered. A

south-westerly wind had sprung up, and dark clouds
were coming up from that direction. There was a
sough in the withy heads on the banks, and the rushes
and flags crackled as they swayed with the breeze. I
at once started for home, and as I went I thought of
the strange coincidence that had introduced me at once
to the principal actors in the drama which I had
listened to the night before—the miller, his daughter,
and last, but not least, "the silver trout."

When I got back, I found Jack Leslie on the lawn
busily putting his rod together. I did the same, for
he had brought my tackle down as well. He asked me
where I had been, and I answered, somewhat reticently,
that I had strolled down to look at the river, and to
see if the fish were feeding.

What a fishing morning it was, as we stepped out
on the gravel path after breakfast. The weather had
now assumed that aspect which the fly-fisherman
always prays for, and but seldom gets—a warm, south-
westerly wind, with driving showers, alternate darkness
and sunshine.

"Now, old man," said Jack, "there is little to
choose as to water, only that the lower half has the
advantage of the mill-head ; but as I think we'd better
not touch that—at any rate, on the first day—after
what Joshua told us last night, you'd better go to the
head of the water, and I'll take the lower bit."

"Oh, no," I replied; "we'll do as we always do,

and toss." For I had determined to fish that mill-head, and to learn a little more, if possible, of the miller and his daughter.

"Call!" cried Jack, as the coin went spinning in the air. For once I felt nervous.

"Woman, it is."

"You're right; well, of course, you'll go to the top." .

"Not a bit of it. I fancy that about the middle of the day I shall want to make a sketch of the old mill, as I shall be tired by that time ; so go ahead, old chap, and we'll meet at lunch time."

"All right, we can change to-morrow; meanwhile, here we are about the middle of the water, only I rather think I've got the better of you, for the mill-head and the meadow above take a good slice of water away, so I ought to show more fish than you at lunch time ; but mind, don't fish the meadow or the mill-head; we'll do that when I've had a chat with old Tomlin. *Au revoir.*"

I watched Jack Leslie, as he left me, swishing his rod and whistling the "Flowers in the Spring," from the *Mikado*, and then I made my way to the river.

The fish were rising everywhere, and the Olive Duns were coming down in myriads, whilst here and there an Alder fly flopped heavily on the water. It is a curious fact that on large rivers the Alder is comparatively small, whilst on small rivers or streams it

2

is generally large, at least so it has always seemed to me.

The very sight of those rising fish—and some of them looked heavy ones—filled me with excitement and increased my desire to catch them. The miller and his daughter, the Silver Trout, and old Joshua's story, all gave way to 'the one prominent feature—fishing. Besides, Jack Leslie had gone, as he said, to the best water, and, good or bad water, had I not forgotten as much as Jack Leslie ever knew about trout fishing, and so I stood upon the bank with a double-handed trout rod in my hand, taking stock of the river and its surroundings.

I may be wrong, and am always open to practical conviction; but, on such a river as I was fishing, and, indeed, on any of the streams in the home counties, I am confident that a double-handed rod is the proper implement. My reason is I can stand farther back from the bank, and so command the water; and that when the line is thrown the length of the rod enables me to keep clear of teazels, or what not, that encumber the bank nearest to me.

How often have I stolen up, crawling and creeping, to a rising fish with a single-handed rod, and, when almost within reach, have been caught up in a teazel and had to extricate the line at the cost of scaring the fish, while with a double-handed rod, say of 14 feet, this ought never to occur.

I scanned the water carefully before putting up my cast, and it seemed to me as if I could do no better than mount the Olive Dun at the end of a fine gut collar, which was stained with green baize. I selected what I considered as perfect an imitation of that ephemera as fur and feathers could represent. A fish was rising under the bank immediately opposite to me, and I put the fly over it in a delicate and gingerly manner—not a stir; twice it went sailing over its very nose—never a move. The fourth time the fish rose almost immediately after the fly had passed, clearly proving that I had not scared it by any previous operations. However, it was evident this was not the fly. Just then a shower came on, and suddenly the fish stopped rising; the surface of the river, which a moment before had been covered with circles, was now completely tranquil.

I sat down, and as I did so an Alder fly lumbered on to my cheek. Perhaps *this* is it, thought I; and on went an Alder.

Now, I have seen Alders and Alders, but, except amongst my personal friends, never have I seen them tied after my own fancy. For the benefit of my readers, I give them the pattern:—Body, orange floss silk, over which a bronze Peacock herl is twisted, so as to leave the orange floss silk visible between each two turns, a small portion of the silk being left at the tail, but not as a tag. Wings taken from the Bustard,

2 *

matched to the colour of the natural fly and dressed flat. Horns, two strands of a soft black hackle.*

Much as I love the fly, on this particular occasion it was no good. I tried hard over every rising fish; no go. What, then, were they rising at? The problem was soon solved, though by accident. Whilst in the act of creeping up to a rising fish I kicked against a bunch of rushes and flags, out of which fluttered a heavy, light-coloured fly, which, taken by the wind, dropped into the middle of the river, and was immediately seized. I soon caught another, and found it to be the Sedge fly. On went the Sedge, and two minutes after I had the satisfaction of drinking the health of a lovely two-pound trout as it lay in the bottom of my landing-net.

Then commenced the fun. After each shower the fish rose freely, and stopped the moment the rain-drops pattered on the water. Unconsciously, I approached the prohibited ground, the meadow next to the mill-head. As I clambered over the fence I marked a heavy fish down close to the opposite bank immediately under an old pollard. " That 's a whopper," I mentally exclaimed, "and if there is any virtue in 'fine and far' I 'll add you to my basket."

A slight detour into the meadow brought me a little below and opposite to the fish ; down I went on my

---

* Dressed by Bernard, Church Place, Piccadilly.

knees, and as I did so the trout rose again. The moment the fly went over it up it came and I struck, but the line came back without the welcome strain; that I had not touched it I felt certain; would it come again? I let it rest for a couple of minutes, during which time I saw no signs of the fish, and then, trembling with excitement, I once more cast over the spot.

This time the hook went home, and with a shake of the head and a heavy roll away went the trout down stream. Across the water at the end of the meadow a chain had been stretched, and it was evident, if I could not stop the fish before it got there, I must lose it; but to arrest the career of a 5 lbs. trout—as I felt certain this one must, at least, be—was no easy matter. Whizz went the winch, my good old greenheart rod was bending almost double, and still the fish made for the chain, which, to add to my difficulties, was covered with weeds.

I dared not show the butt any more, and began to despair of the capture, when the fish suddenly stopped, and came racing back up stream like a mad fellow; so fast, indeed, that I had to run back into the meadow in order to keep a tight line.

The cause of this mad rush was soon explained. Coming through the gate on the opposite side was the same young girl I had seen in the morning with the old miller, and in her white muslin dress and large Leghorn hat, with a background of pale green willows,

she made as fair a picture as one would wish to look
upon. Her entry upon the scene had, for the moment,
diverted my attention, although, with true Fisherman's
instinct, I still kept a tight line upon the fish.

"He 'll be into the weeds in a minute, if you don't
mind," cried a tuneful voice, "you 've got hold of one
of the big ones"; and then she went on excitedly,
"I 'm sure you won't be able to land him yourself;
I 'll be round in a minute," and off she went back
again through the gate.

Well, thought I, this is an adventure with a ven-
geance; and then the tug tug, jigger jigger of the fish
reminded me I had something else to think of; besides,
what a mortification it would be to lose the fish under
such conditions. Just then Dora Tomlin joined me,
having possessed herself of my landing net, which was
sticking up in the next meadow.

"I used to be a good hand, Sir, with a landing net,"
she commenced, in a sort of apologetic manner, "and I
felt sure you would not be able to land that fish without someone, and so I—and so—but perhaps you 'd
rather—" and she blushed and stammered.

I proceeded at once to explain to Miss Tomlin how
glad I was of her assistance, that nothing on earth
should induce me to take that fish without her aid. I
think, in my confusion, I told her that I was always in
the habit of having a lady to land my fish, and much
preferred them to a keeper or male attendant, and was

going on in a like strain, when she stopped me with—
" There ! he 's making for the old pollard stump.
Take care, or you 'll lose him."

The extra pressure I put on brought the fish up, and
it sprang into the air, showing its noble proportions.

" What a beauty ! " exclaimed my companion. " I
hope you won 't lose him."

The fish was now getting tired, and, marking a clean
spot just below where I was standing, I coaxed it down
stream. What was my surprise to see Miss Tomlin,
without a word of instruction, get below the fish, drop
the net into the water, and wait until, exhausted and
gasping, I brought it within reach. Then, without the
slightest hurry, she slipped the net under, and landed
the trout on the bank.

That I was not only delighted and surprised goes
without saying, and whilst admiring my capture, I expressed a hope that I was not trespassing, as I now,
for the first time, observed the locality I was in. This
led to a conversation and to a mutual introduction.
When my fair companion heard that I was an artist
her delight knew no bounds. Would I paint a picture
of the mill ? and would I let her watch me while doing
so ? and would I mind her asking me not to fish the
mill-head ? It was a whim of her father's who was not
very well. If she 'd asked me to stand on my head in
the middle of the river I should have done so at once,
I think. Somehow or another we had seated ourselves

upon the bank, and the finest trout in the world would have had no attractions for me, nor do I think I should have thought anything more about fishing had not a " halloo" in the distance warned me that I was on earth with mortals and not in heaven with an angel, and that that mortal was Jack Leslie. She heard it too, and, getting up, wished me good day with a sweet smile, adding :

" I lost my brooch the other day, leaning out of the boat on the other side, just opposite here, when the water was muddy, and so I came to look for it to-day."

As she was going I ventured to ask permission to call upon her and show her some of my sketches, which she granted, and so we parted.

A few minutes after Jack appeared with five and a half brace of trout. I had only one and a half brace. Did I tell him the reason ? No, dear reader. Would you ?

It was very lucky for me that Jack's eye was fixed upon my last capture. If he had not been intent upon admiring the proportions of that fish he could not have failed to perceive the flutter of a white muslin skirt in the next meadow, as it disappeared in the direction of the mill. As for me, I became suddenly intent upon unpacking the contents of the luncheon basket.

" I say, old man," said Jack, suddenly turning upon me, " I thought we had agreed that you were not to fish this meadow."

" Well, yes," I replied, mendaciously fishing out a

lettuce from the bottom of the basket ; " but, you see, I don't know the water as well as you do ; and I saw this beggar rising, and I really did not stop to look at the locality—come on, let's have lunch. '

" All right, old man," and, coming towards me, he remarked : "That's about as perfect a specimen of the *Salmo fario* as has ever been taken out of these waters. How the dickens did you land it ? What the devil is this ?" he queried, stooping to pick up a lady's glove, with eight buttons.

Of course, if that glove had had only one button, or even two, I might have found an excuse ; but, no, this one seemed to me to have about forty. The situation was rather awkward. " By Jove ! it *is* a lady's glove," I ventured, looking at it as if I'd never seen such a thing before. " What a lot of buttons it's got, and—and what a little one ! "

" Yes," said Jack drily, and looking me straight in the face, " my impression is the same. It *is* a lady's glove."

" Well, never mind what it is. I'm awfully hungry ; come on." I at once proceeded to demolish the wing of a chicken.

That brute Jack stuck that delicate and adorable glove on the top of a thistle, and gave a prolonged whistle that irritated me : it was not so much the whistle as the way in which he looked at the glove and then at me when he did so.

"I suppose it will be the correct thing," I ventured, "to give that fish to the miller, won't it?"

"Yes, I'll send the boy down with it, with my compliments," he replied, opening a bottle of Bass.

"You'll send it? Confound it! I caught it, and I ought to take it."

"But you don't know the miller and there'll be a row; besides, I shall be able to take this glove down at the same time. I fancy it must belong to Miss Tomlin; so while you go and fish the upper water after lunch, I'll stroll on down to the mill and apologise for your trespassing."

I was very fond of Jack Leslie, and would have done anything in the world for him, but this was too much.

That Miss Tomlin should have her glove returned by anyone else than myself I could not for a moment endure, and so I said, with as much equanimity as possible, "Well, all right, you take the fish and I'll take the glove."

"Why?" he retorted, and there was a world of meaning in the query.

"Division of labour, you know. Besides, I want to make Mr. Tomlin's aquaintance; I want to ask permission to make a study of the mill, and then, you know, you said you'd arrange for me to have a throw on the mill-head, and with this wind there must be a fine curl on it. Besides, there's no particular hurry, is there? I fancy the lower end here, and, as you seem to have done so well up above, it 's a pity you shouldn't stick to it for the rest of to-day."

Jack Leslie got up without answering a word; he filled his pipe, very carefully, lit it, and then took up his rod, basket and net, and, raising his flask, he said— "Houghton, you go to the top of the class. Here 's your good health," and sauntered off to the upper water.

I employed myself leisurely packing up the *débris* of the lunch, and then despatched the boy with it to the farmhouse. Fortunately there was no one in sight. The glove being still on the thistle, I edged gradually nearer and nearer, and finally, after a furtive glance around, I pounced upon it.

Why I should have taken such an interest in this glove I did not then know. After all, it was only a lady's glove, and all I had to do was to put it in my pocket, go on fishing, and return it when the proper time came. Why I looked at it, smoothed it, and then smelt it, I can't make out; but I did, and then, to tell the truth, I kissed it.

Just at that moment a shower came on, and I hid the precious gauntlet in my bosom, taking refuge under the hedge. The shower passed, the fish began to rise again, but the river had no longer any charms for me. I took up my rod almost mechanically and sauntered to the edge of the stream. Heavy waves rolled over the shallows, as the fish started on catching

sight of me, but I heeded nothing. I lazily flicked the
fly on to the water without aim or reason. I was
thinking of Dora Tomlin, of the circumstance that
had brought us together, and as I thought I remembered the incident of the brooch which she had come
to seek. Why should I not look for it ?

Here was an inspiration which was seized with avidity. I flung my old good Blacker rod down. I divested
myself of my coat, fishing basket, &c., and began
cautiously to examine the water. She had indicated
the spot, but, after careful searching, from my side I
could see nothing of it. I must cross, but where ?
The stream was uneven as to depth, and apparently
treacherous as to bottom. I looked up and down ; the
chain was my only chance ; besides, by going below
the spot I should not muddy the water. On reaching
the spot I found there were two chains, one placed
considerably below the water, which seemed to me to
offer the facility I required. I commenced my journey
by placing my feet on the lower chain and grasping
the upper one. All went well till I neared the centre,
when, to my horror, I found the lower chain gradually
giving way. Yes, the water was already trickling in
over the tops of my waders. I struggled, I floundered,
but it was no use, in I went up to my armpits : but,
still grasping the upper chain, I got to the opposite
bank, and crawled up covered with weeds, looking like
a drowned rat.

All the romance of half an hour ago had been washed out of me, and I thought of nothing except my situation if Jack Leslie should return, or even Dora Tomlin. I pulled off my wading stockings and emptied them, wrung my clothes, and then literally hung myself out to dry. Fortunately, the sun was very warm as I walked briskly up and down the bank to assist the drying process. In my peregrinations I passed the spot where the brooch was supposed to have been dropped. Did my eyes deceive me? No, there was certainly something shining at the tail of that weed, and in less than no time I was in the water and back on the bank, holding triumphantly in my hands a silver brooch, beautifully modelled in the shape of a trout. Had I indeed caught the Silver Trout? and then the prophetic words of old Joshua occurred to me, that "on the day a silver trout was taken out of the river the miller would lose his life and his only daughter."

It was true I had got the brooch and that my clothes and waders were dry enough to put on, but how was I to get back to the other side of the river? I could, of course, go round by the mill, but there I ran the risk of meeting Dora, and, of course, I should have to account for being without my coat, and of necessity return the brooch. Just then I remembered that there was a small foot-bridge, some two meadows up, that I had not thought of, and I at once made my way towards it, all the while ruminating as to what I should do with the brooch and whether I should tell Jack Leslie anything about it. Then there was the glove business; what was I to do about that? I was prepared to be most unmercifully chaffed by Jack; that I knew was inevitable, but how to get out of the business without compromising myself, I knew not.

Pondering on these matters, I arrived at the foot-bridge and was about to cross, when a roar of laughter caused me to look up, and there, as ill-luck would have it, was Jack Leslie, fishing in the adjoining meadow.

"What on earth is up now? and what are you doing without your coat?"

As a rule I am not in want of an answer under any ordinary situation, but this was a poser. Jack Leslie came towards me, and I braced myself to meet the situation.

"What are you doing on that side of the river, old man; and where the deuce are your coat and traps? What's the matter with you, man? Why don't you answer?" he shouted, as I was hesitating.

"I suppose I am not responsible to you for all my actions," I answered sulkily. "I crossed over the river to look at something I saw on the opposite side."

"Oh, indeed, and to do that you took off your coat and went round by the mill, I suppose?"

"No, I didn't go round by the mill—But there,

don't bother, Jack, that's a good fellow. Fact is, I fell into the river trying to cross by the chain, and I'm going home to change. By Jove! Look at that lovely fish feeding under the willow. You are a duffer if you can't catch him!"

In a moment Jack had forgotten everything, and I left him creeping up the bank intent on the capture of that trout, whilst I made my way to where I had left my traps. Arriving at the spot I at once determined to return to the farmhouse and change my clothes, and as I went I questioned myself as to what was the meaning of the interest I felt in this miller's daughter. What was she to me? Hadn't I seen lots of pretty girls—much prettier than Dora, and yet I had never bestowed as much thought upon them as I had upon Dora—Dora! The very name sounded so soft as I whispered it to the summer wind. Yes, Dora was an awfully pretty name!

I walked slowly back to the farm. Under usual circumstances, had I been going to change my clothes, I should have used much more dispatch, but now, somehow, I felt as if I didn't care to get back to my fishing. What! not go back to the river? Why, what had come over me? Trout-fishing was the one dream of my life, as I painted away in my dreary studio; a day's trouting was looked forward to and prepared for weeks before; but to-day, somehow, I thought I was tired—that I had fished enough for the first day;

that my waders were not dry, and, in fact, that I would fish no more that day.

But I was not too tired to take a canvas, my colour-box, sketching easel and umbrella, and walk back to the old mill at the rate of five miles an hour. Now I did not particularly want that umbrella, as there were plenty of trees, but it occurred to me that a white umbrella stuck in a conspicuous place on the bank of the mill-head must attract attention from the mill. Yes, probably the miller's boy will come out and see what it was, or the cook, or the gardener, and then, perhaps —well, we would see.

I planted myself in the most open spot, and in full view of the window of the miller's house. I placed my canvas on the easel, and I commenced sketching the outline of the mill. Somehow or another my eyes were more often kept upon those windows than upon my canvas, and the perspective of the lines I had already traced were most wofully out of drawing. Just then the old miller appeared in the porch, followed by his daughter. Were they coming this way? My heart was absolutely thumping against my ribs. Yes, they were coming. What should I do? What should I say? As they approached, I felt I was blushing like a boy.

"You see, Miss Tomlin, that I have taken advantage as soon as possible of the permission given me, and have left Mr. Leslie to fish by himself."

" You are quite welcome, Sir. Indeed, any friend of
Mr. Leslie's is always welcomed here."

A sudden thought flashed across my brain. Could
I have made a mistake? Was the girl who had crept
into my heart in so short a time also beloved by my
friend? And why not? Had not Jack known them
for years? Could anyone see Dora Tomlin and know
her without loving her? I must be mad—I was a fool,
a dolt, an idiot. Miss Tomlin interrupted my thoughts
by introducing me to her father, at the same time
adding, " He is not quite right in his mind, and takes
you for someone else; pray humour him."

I bowed, scarcely knowing what to do or what to
say. The old man seemed to take no notice of me;
but, keeping his eyes fixed on the water, muttered:
" The time is near; I am coming, wife. The captain
is here. He has come at last, but he is alone. It is
better, wife, to hide our shame." Then, turning to
me, he said, abruptly :

"Why did you stop away so long, and where is she?"

Dora answered, "Dear father, this is Mr. Haughton,
a friend of Mr. Leslie's."

The old man passed his hand across his forehead, and
then, coming to me, held out his hand, and, in a
rational voice, he said, " You are welcome, Sir. Indeed,
any friend of Mr. Leslie's is always welcomed. I hope
you have had good sport? There are plenty of fish,
and good ones, if you can catch them."

"Oh! Mr. Haughton," cried Dora, "are you going to begin to paint; because, if so, I should like to stop and watch you—that is, if I may?"

Half an hour ago, had Dora asked me that, I should have replied in quite a different way; but that speech of hers about Jack Leslie rankled in my mind. "Certainly, Miss Tomlin," I said, "if you wish it; but, to tell you the truth, I don't feel up to work, and I was on the point of stopping as, somehow or another, I cannot draw to-day."

"Then perhaps you will join us in a cup of tea; it is about time. Your things will be all safe here," and, in a lower tone, added, "You must not mind father. He has suffered a great deal, as I daresay Mr. Leslie told you. Will you come?"

There was nothing for it; I had better go. Besides, I could return the glove and the brooch, and see what effect that might have, and so I followed Dora Tomlin and her father into the cosiest of parlours, full of woman's surroundings and occupations, with the sweet scent of flowers coming through the windows and the urn steaming upon the table. I must confess I felt a sort of tightness at the heart as I watched Dora Tomlin's graceful figure presiding over the tea-table. Could there be anything between her and Jack? That was the all-absorbing question.

"I expect Mr. Leslie in to tea," she remarked quietly.

"Do you really?" I answered, hardly knowing what I did say.

"Yes, he generally comes in before the evening fishing, as he calls it."

Well! what was there in that? Why shouldn't he come in to tea in the same way that I had? Just then Jack passed the window.

"Ah! here he is; I thought he wouldn't forget tea-time."

As Jack Leslie entered the room the old miller was seated upon a couch close to the window, looking out on to the mill-head. Dora was at the tea-table and I was leaning against the mantel-piece. I see the picture now. Jack paused at the door.

"Well, I'm sure," he cried, "you have not taken long to make acquaintance. I looked for you as I came down the river, for the purpose of bringing you in and introducing you, but I see that's unnecessary. May I venture to inquire how this came about?"

"Presently, *Jack*," answered Dora. "Sit down and have your tea."

Jack! She called him *Jack!* It was all over. My romance was gone. That one word had shattered my hope, my dream, and Dora was no more to me at that moment than any other girl. I made up my mind at once.

"Well, you see, Jack," I said, "I came down to sketch, was invited by Miss Tomlin to tea, and I

3 *

thought I would take the opportunity of returning her a glove she had lost whilst landing my trout for me, and a brooch I found which must be hers."

Jack indulged in a prolonged whistle.

" A brooch, did you say? " cried Dora.

" Yes, a Silver Trout."

" A Silver Trout ! " cried the old miller, springing to his feet. "Who knows anything about ' the Silver Trout'? Did you say you had caught the Silver Trout? Do you know what you have done ? You have committed murder, cold-blooded murder ; you are an assassin ; you—you "—and the old man fell back upon the couch gasping for breath.

We were at once by his side. The bell was rung and a man sent immediately for the doctor. The old miller lay insensible, a small stream of blood trickling slowly from his lips. Gradually his eyes opened, and were fixed upon Dora and Jack.

" Lift me up," he murmured. " It has come true. I knew it." Then taking Dora's hand, he placed it in Jack's. "Take care of her Jack—The Silver Trout. I am coming, darling wife ; I am coming, to you," and sank back a corpse.

I have little more to add. I was terribly shocked at having been the innocent cause of such a catastrophe, and to my dying day shall never forget it. It is needless to say that Jack explained to me afterwards the situation. How he had wooed and won Dora long ago, and how he had intended to tell me all about it at supper in the evening. And so the legend came true. The day that a Silver Trout was taken out of the river the miller would lose his life and his only daughter.

THE MAN WITH THE GREEN BOX.

I HAVE heard that the famous saying attributed to Dr. Johnson, when describing an angler, "A worm at one end and a fool at the other," was not written by that worthy and astute philosopher at all. Well, all I can say is that if he had said a fly at one end and fool at the other, it would be more applicable to my case. Now, I want to be quite plain with my readers, as plain as my wife says I am, and as plain as the fishing I understand. I have always been fond of fishing ever since I was a very small lad. In those days the Paddington Canal, the Serpentine, the Ornamental Water in Kensington Gardens, and the ponds about Hampstead and Highgate were my fishing grounds, and for the moment I was content.

Unfortunately, one Christmas my father, who was a carpenter, gave me a box. I 've got that box still, and

even now it contains the remains of old chrysalises, dried
up and mummy-like ends of worms, split float caps,
odd pieces of gut, rusty hooks, fish scales, and such-like
mouldering piscatorial reminiscences.   I don't believe
there's money enough in the world to tempt me to part
with that dear old green box—for, of course, it was
painted green—with its narrow strap, that has many a
time cut my shoulders to pieces, not with the weight
of fish within it, but with the impedimenta in the
shape of tackle and bait which I considered it necessary
to stow in its multitudinous trays and divisions.   I've
had a good mind to send that box some of these days,
to put in the window of *Land and Water*.   Well, of
course, after getting this box, and my uncle having
given me two rods, I abandoned my old fishing
localities and sought pastures new and more worthy of
such a fit-out.   These were the lower waters of the
Lea, and the New River from Broxbourn down, with
an occasional day on the Reservoir at Cheshunt, the
Welsh Harp, and the Thames as far as Kingston.

My father wanted me to follow his trade, but I did
not seem to take to it, first of all because the hours were
too long, and would curtail my piscatorial pursuits;
and secondly, because I was in love, and *she* did not
approve of a carpenter for a husband. So, after a good
deal of trouble, I got a situation in the city in a large
wholesale leather house, where I laboured very hard
for nigh on to thirty years, never neglecting my fish-

ing, and eventually becoming the head of the firm, with plenty of time and plenty of money to prosecute my predilections for the river side.

In the meantime I had married. My wife did not approve of my love of fishing, and upon one occasion we were very near a separation, when I heard her give an order to the servant to light the kitchen fire with that "nasty green box." It was then that the blood of the Joneses was aroused. What! burn my green fishing-box, the companion of my earliest fishing excursions; that box—which, by the way, was about the size of an ordinary portmanteau—that I had treasured for so many years, upon whose lid, whilst seated on the bank, I had caught innumerable colds and very few fish. It was too much. I am not going to relate the language I used upon that occasion, but the box was *not* burnt.

Of course, all this while I read with avidity the columns of those periodicals devoted to fishing. I went down to the Thames regularly on April 1 to try for a trout, which, I may say, I have never caught. I joined an angling club, and became vice-chairman. I could not sing or make a speech, or else I'm sure I should have been made chairman. I bought some pictures by Rolfe; I had the largest of my fish stuffed, and I once wrote a fishing song, which I got somebody else to sing at the monthly meeting of our society.

I soon began to be known as "The Man with the Green Box"—that is, in the immediate neighbourhood

of London; and once—yes, perish the day!—I went to
have a day's trout-fishing in Hampshire with one of
our customers, and from that day the usual placid
and satisfactory results of my piscatorial wanderings
received a rude shock.

Hinc illæ lachrymæ.

My friend was an enthusiastic fisherman—that is to
say, from his point of view. The only fishes he cared
to angle for were the lordly salmon or plucky trout.
It is true, I had ventured occasionally to allow my
mind to wander upon such topics, but I had always
nipped those ideas in the bud, as being far too high a
flight for my means or my ability. Throw a fly! Why,
it had taken me two years of hard labour to cast a spinning bait decently, and then five to put a bait, much
less a bleak, upon a flight of hooks and make it spin,
and then considerable time to " travel " for chub with
Nottingham tackle, and now to cast a fly! Mercy! I
fancied I could hear the whiplike crack of the gut as
my fly was lost at every swish of the rod. Oh, no,
coarse-fishing was good enough for me—and yet, and
yet, well, why shouldn't I try? and so I accepted my
friend's invitation.

I bought a fly rod with sundry misgivings as I tried
its capacity, very awkwardly and much to the amusement of the fishing-tackle maker. I bought a book of
flies with their names on each page and the months

they were used for, a round tin box for casting lines, and a basket. I got up very early every morning and I went into the back garden to practise, and I succeeded in breaking both top joints of my rod, two panes of glass in the kitchen window, hooking a favourite fowl of my wife's, that gave me the best sport with the fly, up to the present time; I have ever had, spraining my wrist, and giving myself such a pain in the back that lumbago was a joke to it.

Well, the eventful day came and I met my friend at the Waterloo Station. I had some slight hopes that upon this auspicious occasion some members of our society might have been on the platform to see me off. It would have looked well, I thought; but no, there was no one there, and, in addition, I was half an hour too early. Never mind. I contemplated my fishing paraphernalia, as it was heaped up on the platform, with intense satisfaction. The green box was there. What! do you think I'd have gone without it? Perish the thought. And so was my bundle of rods for coarse-fishing, resting lovingly on its lid. For, argued I, perhaps I mayn't get on with the trout, and then surely there'll be some eddy were I can, at any rate, find some coarse fish. I took up the basket, and put it on; I thought I looked better that way; and then I took up the fly-rod in its new case, and then, somehow or another, I felt as if that old green box and bundle of bottom fishing rods didn't look quite respectable, and that I ought not to identify myself with them; so I lounged away. Just then my friend joined me. After shaking hands, his eye suddenly lit on the old green box.

"Some bank fisherman going down to fish the Basingstoke Canal," he remarked, with a curl of the lip, and a short, aggressive laugh.

"I suppose so," I answered at once, making up my mind not to own proprietorship, and as he lounged away I surreptitiously gave a porter sixpence to put them in the baggage van and label them to our destination. I don't think this was quite fair to the old green box, but then you must remember that my friend was not aware that I had never thrown a fly in my life, and if there is a thing an angler is more sensitive about than another, it is to appear not to know all the branches of the gentle art; and so, full of guile, I got into the carriage. It was the first week in May, and our conversation was on this wise :—

HE. "These last few days of warm weather ought to have put the water in good order, and the fly should be up pretty strong."

I. "Yes; I should think the flies must be very strong just now."

HE. "Eh? What do you say?"

I. "Me! I quite agree with you; they ought to be 'very fine and large.'"

He. "Ah! capital. I suppose, as usual, we shall find the iron-blue dun in myriads."

I. "I should say so, too," not having the remotest conception what he was talking about.

He. "I hope you have brought a double-handed rod; you want to fish far and fine on this water."

I. "Oh! I think I've got what will do." My heart going into my boots at the reminiscence of the back yard, and the difficulty I had to get ten yards out.

He. "I told the keeper to meet us, and, as you don't know the water, he'd better go with you."

I. "D—— the keeper—I mean, if you don't mind, I'd rather go by myself. You see, I like being alone when I am fly-fishing."

He. "Oh! I see. Sly dog. But I'll keep my eye on you."

I. "Will you? Well, I don't think that's fair. I think our pitches ought to be quite wide apart."

He. "Pitches! What on earth do you mean?"

Just then the train came into a station, and, I am thankful to say, further conversation was interrupted, several people getting into our compartment. My mind, too, was exercised as to what I should do about my box and bundle of rods, and, whilst deliberating on this, we arrived at our destination.

Yes! the arrival of that train was fortunate and opportune. I had made up my mind what to do. Of course I must wire to my wife as to my safe arrival and to do this I must of necessity go into the telegraph-office. There was my chance to get rid of that green box. But unfortunately, as we stepped out of our compartment my friend's malcontent eye was fixed on the green box; it had just been put on the platform. "Confound it!" he cried, "here's that fellow come down here. What does he want! Oh! well, I suppose some private carp pond, or something of that kind, for, of course, the very idea of anything but the legitimate was gall and wormwood to my friend's high-flown piscatorial ideas. I must say I suffered between the desire to hold up the prestige of my old green box and to sever my connection with it altogether as entirely opposed to my now advanced ideas of fishing. I got to that telegraph office, and, what between my anxiety that no harm should happen to my *bête noir*, or rather green, and that my friend should not see the *ruse*, I hardly knew whether I stood on my head or my heels. I wired: "Green box all right; don't know what to do with it." I believe, when my wife got that wire, she had a strong fit of hysterics—at least, I know that the spirit case suffered. As I came out of the telegraph-office, I saw my friend talking to a tall, thin man in velveteen coat, with long leather leggings up to his waist, and a lot of flies stuck in the top of his hat. The moment I saw that man I felt him to be my natural enemy; and, as I glared at him, I *knew* he was the keeper. They went into the refreshment-room, and now was my opportunity. I got hold of a porter, and told him to send the box, with the rods, by the first opportunity down to the hotel, and say that a gentleman would call for them. Then I lounged into the refreshment-room and joined my friend and the keeper.

" Ah ! here you are," he said. " What will you have ? This is the keeper, and he tells me the water is in splendid order, and, as I expected, the fly is very strong."

The man with the leggings touched his hat looked me all over, and I am almost sure that he smiled, and an evil smile it was. However, I thought I 'd better make friends and perhaps put on a little " side," so I casually remarked that I was glad to hear about the flies, as I had found that when the flies were strong the fish were, as a rule, equally fine and larger. At that he burst into a loud laugh, then I felt a cold shiver go down my back, and wished myself on the banks of the lake at the Welsh Harp, or anywhere but where I was. How I hated that man. At last we got into a fly and drove to the hotel. My friend got down first and went into the hotel. I was following, when I heard him give a shout, and as I entered the door the cause of that shout was explained. There was my green box, with the bundle of rods, in the middle of the hall. The keeper followed me in, and he, too, went up to examine it.

"What the deuce is the meaning of this?" my friend said. "That confounded box has followed us everywhere. Who does it belong to? And what the devil can he mean by bringing such tackle down to the Itchen?" examining the rods.

"Well," suggested the keeper, "perhaps he's going to swim a worm for grayling, but not on my water, if I knows it ; and where else he can go I don't know, unless it be on the miller's bit, and if I catch him trying that game on, I'll make it hot for him. Why, Sir," said he, looking me straight in the face, "we caught one of these London bank fisherman a-trying that sort of thing here last season, and what do you think we did to him?"

I expressed my inability to form any opinion as to what should be done in such a case.

"Well, Sir, we made him swallow his bag of worms. He ! he !"

"Good gracious !" I exclaimed, "you ought to have been well punished."

"Oh ! not a bit, Sir. Anybody who tries bait-fishing on the Itchen gets no sympathy from anyone down here."

"Well, confound the box !" cried my friend, " we are wasting time. Let's get down to the water."

My hour was come ; now for it. I don't think, in the whole course of my life, I ever hated the bank of a river as much I did that bank of the Itchen on that

day. I put my rod together in a sort of dazed state,
the keeper wanted to help me, but I refused his assistance, so he went to my friend. I ran the line through
the rings, and then I pondered what to do. I lit a
cigar and watched my friend. He was choosing a fly
out of his box—good; of course I must do that, but
what fly? Oh! to be sure, had I not got my fly-book,
with the names of the flies written against them? Of
course, it was quite easy. I looked up May. I saw
yellow dun and red spinner, also hare's-ear dun. I
looked at the water, and I tried to see the flies that
were so strong, but I couldn't see anything. Just then
the keeper came to me and said, pointing to the
opposite bank :

"There's a grand fish feeding at the tail of that weed,
Sir."

"Is there?" said I. "Well, let him feed; it will
do him good. I don't want to disturb him."

"Beg pardon, Sir," said the keeper, "I don't quite
understand? I was telling you there was fish feeding
at—— There he is, Sir! He must be a good three
pound. You can just reach him nicely."

"Well, but I think my friend ought to have first
chance ; besides, I'm not quite ready. You go and tell
him."

I thought that was a good stroke, and the moment
the keeper's back was turned I extricated a fly from
my book, which was in the pocket, labelled "Yellow

Dun." I couldn't see anything yellow about the fly; on the contrary, it had white wings and a bronzy body. However, there it was, so I attached it to the end of my reel line, and then I betook myself down the river's side as far from my friend as possible, with the advantage of a high hedge intervening. What happened to me there will be told the reader, upon the distinct understanding that it is kept a perfect secret between us, for if it were to come to the ears of any member of our Piscatorial Society, I feel sure I should be asked to resign.

Yes! that hedgerow was a vantage coign for me. I could, in the first place, not only hide my operations from my friends and that fellow with the leggings, but I could also watch what *they* did and act accordingly. Now, when I say "act," I mean that in such a situation no one could blame me for endeavouring to look as little like the fool I really felt. The only way that I can account for putting myself into such a situation is, as I before remarked, the innate dislike that anyone aspiring to piscatorial honours has of showing a want of knowledge upon angling subjects generally. As I gazed upon the river and then peeped through the hedge, I thought to myself how much better it would have been had I, in the first instance, made a clean breast of it and acknowledged my inability and my utter want of knowledge of even the common rudiments of fly-fishing. Then, too, there was that box—

4

the fatal green box. Well, no matter! I must face it out now. Was I not vice-chairman of the "Friendly Bumble Bee Anglers"? Of course I was, and under the circumstances—perish the thought of my taking a back seat; and so I peered through the hedge. This is what I saw :—

My friend was crawling upon his knees towards a bit of long grass, rushes and what not that grew upon the bank. The man with the leggings was on his knees holding the landing-net. My friend, as he crawled backwards and forwards, was swishing his rod, what for I couldn't imagine, though it reminded me of my rehearsal in our back yard. Then, all of a sudden, the point of his rod was lowered, and as he raised it again I distinctly heard an exclamation. He's got him, thought I, and I began to get excited, but no, the rod remained stationary and did not bend. Then the man with the leggings commenced crawling on his stomach up to the bank, and then I knew my friend was hung up in a teazle or bush. There was a good deal of fumbling, a great many muttered curses, before the keeper had crawled back again and my friend had repaired damages. Well, thought I, this isn't half as good fun as sitting on my old green box watching my float travel over a well-baited swim, besides crawling— goodness! I weigh over eighteen stone, and my physical proportions are not adapted to such acrobatic performances. "If I must do that, I'll give it up," I said to myself. Just then I heard someone whistling the " British Grenadiers," and, looking down the river, I saw a boy coming along, his hands in his pockets, and making straight for me. At the same moment, too, my eyes caught sight of a shed in the field, and a sudden inspiration seized me. I put down my rod and advanced to meet him. He was not a pleasant-looking boy, but he appeared guileless, and I think he had the thickest and biggest boots on I ever saw.

" Good morning," said I, quite familiarly.

" How do, Sir," replied he, making a sort of upward movement of his hand.

" Want to earn a shilling ? " I queried.

" He ! he ! " was the answer.

" Oh ! you don't ? "

" Yes, but I do, mister."

" Well," said I, " you go to the hotel in the village, take this note to the landlord, and he 'll give you a green box and a bundle of rods. You bring them down to that shed, and wait there for me."

" Ees, Sir," he said, about to depart.

" And remember," I added, " don 't you let anyone see you till I come, or you won 't get that shilling."

" Ees, Sir "—and he was gone.

Now this was my inspiration. I knew very well that I could not do anything in the fly-fishing line, and I also knew that I had a lot of brandlings beautifully scoured in a flannel bag in the green box. If I could circumvent my friend and the keeper, I should, I thought, not go back empty-handed ; and if they caught me—well, all I could do would be to make a clean breast of it, and defy the keeper to make me swallow my bag of worms. In the meantime, I must endeavour to do the best I could, and at any hazard. get rid of them.

Just then a shout came from the other side of the hedge, and, looking through, I saw my friend had hooked the fish. I scrambled through, tearing my trousers and falling into the ditch on the other side ; panting, muddy, and bleeding I arrived on the spot and witnessed the struggle. In my excitement I rushed at the keeper and tried to take the landing-net away ; this the " Leather Stocking" resented.

"Let me land him," I appealed to my friend.

"Certainly, give Mr. Jones the net."

Never shall I forget the moment ; the fish was nearly done, and I could see his broad, speckled side and yellow belly as he turned up in his last struggles. I seized the landing net, and rushed to the bank.

"Easy ! easy ! get below him " ; but no, there he was, the first trout I'd ever seen caught. Just then the bank gave way and I slid in up to my middle.

"Confound it ! Look out, or you'll break the cast."

But no, my soul was in arms and eager for the fray. I dashed the landing-net at his head, the gut parted, and I sat down in the river up to my armpits. Oh !

horror. That keeper pulled me out, and the remark he made I shall never forget. My friend, who is good-natured, simply said, "D——n it." I said nothing. Picture !

Of course, being wet through, there was nothing to be done but to go back to the hotel and change, so making all sorts of excuses to my friend, and telling him I would follow him and he was not to stop, I put my rod in a safe place and returned to the hotel, and as I went I thought that some men's adversity was other men's opportunity ; and here was mine, for assuredly I would now be able to lose my friend and "Leather Stocking." On my way to the hotel, I am free to confess, I was not much in love with myself. I felt I had suffered in the estimation of my friend and I knew that in the keeper I had a mortal enemy. On my way I met my boy with the " green box " and the rods, and I stopped for a moment to give him his directions, and also to take a little refreshment from my flask. It was then I was first struck by the originality of his remarks. This is what occurred. After partaking, I was screwing on the top of the flask, when he said :

" I suppose you don 't know I 'm a teetotaller ? "

Thinking this was meant by way of reproach, I handed him my flask.

" Oh no, thank 'ee ; I don 't drink nothing but milk ! "

I apologised. A pause.

"I suppose you don't know my father died of a broken heart?"

I confessed my ignorance, and said I felt very sorry, upon which, without any further remark, he got up, and, as he shouldered the green box, said:

"I suppose I'll meet you at the shed, and I suppose you won't forget that shilling," and went off whistling "The British Grenadiers."

When I got to the hotel I made the landlord promise he would not say to whom that green box belonged.

After changing my clothes, partaking of some hot port wine negus, and having lit a cigar, I felt more at ease. The only thing that disturbed my mind was as to how I was to use those brandlings, and that without the knowledge of my friend and the lynx-eyed keeper. Well, I would think of some plan on my way back to the river.

On the road I began by trying to remember all the articles I had read on worm-fishing for trout, but the more I pondered the more I thought that such methods as were suggested in those articles were not applicable to a river like the Itchen. Again, I could not fish with a float amongst those long banks of waving weeds. No, that would not do. I remembered Stewart's method; but, then, I had not got any tackle like that. How about a ledger? Ah! that perhaps might work; and

just then I arrived at the shed. About three-quarters
of a mile lower down I could see my friend attended
by the keeper, apparently hard at work. I looked into
the shed, and there was my green box and bundle of
rods sure enough, but the boy was nowhere to be seen.
Going round to the back of the shed his absence was
explained. Running through the meadow, and immediately at the back of the shed, was a small stream
emptying itself into the main river, and about two
hundred yards from its mouth was a lasher of sluice,
doubtless made for damming the water back, so as to
flood the meadows in a spell of dry weather. The little
stream being pretty full, the water was boiling and
seething through an open hatch in the middle of the
sluice, and making quite a little pool below it. From
the constant action of the water against the soft soil of
either bank this had been widened out into a hole of
some fifteen or twenty yards across. Close to the edge
of this hole, kneeling with his back towards me, was
my quondam attendant, the "Suppositionist." In his
hand he held a hazel stick, some six feet in length, to
which, as far as I could see, was attached a piece of
string. His actions denoted the greatest caution. He
would first peer round the corner of the shed in the
direction of the hotel, and would then look towards the
spot where my friend was fishing. Then he would
raise the hazel stick and swing the attachment into the
hole in front of him. "Well," thought I, "*I suppose*

he must be fishing;" and I was about to call to him, when I saw the stick bend; there was a splashing in the hole, and a minute afterwards a lovely trout was literally hauled out by the head, and lay kicking on the bank. In a moment I was master of the situation, and I felt that I should be in a position to show something of a bag. I still watched his proceedings. Having taken off the fish he placed it carefully out of sight in a bed of nettles, and then proceeded to hide his primitive tackle in the thatch of the shed. Just as he had completed his task, and had whistled the first bars of the "British Grenadiers," a loud cough made him aware of my presence. That boy's face was a picture, and the look of stupidity he put on as I approached was beyond description.

"I suppose you ain't been back long?" he queried.

"About ten minutes," I replied, making straight for the bunch of nettles.

"I suppose you know," he added, endeavouring to intercept me, "that this is a goodish hole for a trout; they works up here from the river."

"I suppose I do," said I, steadily advancing, and, kicking the weeds on one side, I discovered five lovely trout, laying side by side, the last capture just vibrating in the agonies of death.

"Where do these come from?" I asked, looking him straight in the face.

"Why, they be trouts," he replied, looking at them

in the most innocent manner. "I suppose you don't know there was a flood last week, and I suppose they got left on the bank when the water went down."

This was too much. I forgot that I had been proposing to myself the same method. I only remembered that I was vice-chairman of the "Friendly Bumble Bee Anglers' Association," and that I had witnessed an act of deliberate poaching.

"You young vagabond!" I exclaimed; "those fish have only just been freshly caught. Bring me that stick you hid just now under the thatch."

"I supposed you wanted some trout, mister, and they ain't easy to catch," he remarked, with a broad grin, not stirring a step, and taking up the last capture; "but if so be as they're only just caught, perhaps they'll live, I'll put 'em in the river again."

That boy fairly took my breath away.

"Put down the fish at once, Sir, and listen to me. You know, if I were to tell the keeper what I saw just now, what would be the consequence. Now, I don't want to do that, but —— "

"I suppose you don't know my sister died of a broken heart," he blubbered.

So much family distress touched me. Placing my hand on his shoulder, I said, "Bring me that stick and show me how you caught them, and we'll see."

I think he saw determination in my eye, and so, still sobbing, he produced his primitive tackle—a hazel stick, a piece of silk line, a rough bit of lead and a single gut hook, on the end of which still dangled the remains of a worm. It immediately flashed across me that if this boy, with such tackle, could succeed, what sport I could have with finer and more appropriate appliances.

"Now, look here, my boy," said I, "I don't want to be hard upon you, and I *do* want some trout. I've got some splendid worms in that green box, and if you will keep quiet, I'll give you half-a-crown, and I won't tell the keeper what I saw."

"I suppose you don't know, Sir, that I learnt how to catch the trout out of this hole from a famous fisher that came from Lunnon. He always caught 'em that way, and I never said a word, I didn't, only——"

"Only what?"

"Well, I suppose you don't know he gave me *five shillings* ?"

The bargain was then and there sealed and our arrangements made in this wise:—The boy was to climb on to the roof of the shed and give me timely warning of the approach of my friend and the keeper. He was then to return to the hotel with the green box and bundle of rods, and I was to take to my fly-rod and make the best show I could.

In a few minutes I was ready, and stealing down cautiously to the lower portion of the hole I pitched my worm right up under the sluice and let it float down towards me keeping a moderately tight line. About half-way down there was a stoppage, and I felt a sharp tug. I struck smartly, and was in my first trout.

Oh, the joy of that moment! Unfortunately I tried to haul him out on the boy's principle, which resulted in breaking the tackle and smashing the top of my rod. Never mind. What did I care for a thousand tops, so, after repairing damages, I went to work again. I caught two fish, one of 1 lb. and one of 1¾ lbs., and then my sentinel gave me due warning of the return of my friends. Never mind, I had 3½ brace of trout, and I felt in the wildest spirits.

The boy was packed off to the hotel with the box and the rods with instructions to wait my return; the trout was put into my basket, and I once more resumed that, to me implement of torture, my fly-rod.

Of course it now behoved me to make a semblance of fly-fishing. I approached the river proper and commenced operations. In endeavouring to get out my line, I caught in a bush behind; then the fly caught in the back of my coat immediately between my shoulders, so I had to take off my coat to get it out. Then I got round a bush growing on the bank nearest to me and nearly fell into the river in trying to get clear.

All this while the reader must remember that I had omitted to put on a casting line, and had fastened, in the most primitive manner, what I supposed to be a "yellow dun" on to my winch line. The perspiration rolled down my cheeks, my back ached, and, laying down my rod, I sat down in despair.

Then I looked into my basket, and felt comforted. The next evening was to be the weekly meeting of the "Bumble Bees." I would then exhibit my take, and I should feel myself the most important man in the room. Whilst ruminating on these matters my friend joined me.

"What have you done?" he cried.

"Oh, nothing much," I answered, in the most nonchalant tone; "only three and a half brace, and I'm about done up."

"Three and a half brace!" he exclaimed; "good gracious! what fly, eh?"

"The yellow dun," I replied, lazily puffing my cigar.

"Well, that's curious. I've only taken a brace, and I know this river backwards. Let's see them."

"When we get up to the hotel," I answered; "it's getting late, and if you're ready I am."

Whilst talking I had not perceived that the fiend of a keeper had taken up my rod, but an exclamation made me turn round, and then I saw he was examining my tackle. Advancing with the fly in his hand he remarked, dryly, that he never knew a fish to look at a "coachman" so early in the day. My friend, too, observed with a peculiar look, "Why, you've got no casting line." Now it is extraordinary how easily lying comes to one, especially about fishing, so I replied that the last cast I had in my box was lost by a fish running me into the weeds, and that was another reason why I should go back.

" You can take that rod to pieces, keeper," I added, " I 'll stroll back."

But my friend was also tired, and so we left the keeper to bring on the rods, etc., and sauntered back to the hotel. On our way my friend congratulated me on my prowess, and remarked that such a performance in bright weather was simply first-class. I modestly answered it was probably my luck, to which he replied there was no such thing as luck upon the Itchen. I am of his opinion.

As we entered the hotel the landlord met us. He asked if we were ready for dinner, to which I replied in the affirmative.

" I am afraid," he said, " you will have to wait a little, gentlemen, as I have had to provide a little more, not expecting the lady."

" The lady ! " we both exclaimed. I looked at my friend, and he looked at me. " I don't expect any lady," I said.

" No more do I," echoed my friend; " there must be some mistake."

" Beg pardon, Sir, I think not. The lady said she 'd had a telegram about a ' green box,' and I told her it was all right, and it was here."

I could have dropped where I stood. " Where is she ? " I exclaimed wildly.

" In the sitting-room, Sir, waiting for you."

I staggered to the door, closely followed by my friend. I turned the handle and entered, and there, seated in an arm-chair, was Mrs. Jones, my better half, and—how shall I tell it?—the green box beside her ! Tableau.

Well, of course, further concealment was useless. I called for strong brandy and water, and my wife told me not to be a fool. My friend sat down and fairly screamed with laughter, and, to make my cup of misery full, that boy came in and handed me my bag of worms, apologising for his neglect in omitting to do so before. Dear reader, I have not been fly-fishing since—I shall never go again ; and the moral to be learnt from this episode is, I think, obvious :—" Never let your vanity so far get the better of your common sense as to make you ashamed of acknowledging your ignorance."

TROUT-FISHING

IN THE

RHENISH PROVINCES.

———◆———

IT will be unnecessary for me to enter into the
details as to the best route to be taken to reach
the Rhenish provinces from England.   Suffice it
to say that that most excellent publication, *Bradshaw's
Continental Guide,* gives every possible information of
the way to reach Cologne, which should be the place
fixed upon as a starting point.   I have, as nearly as
possible, commenced my narrative in the centre of
these provinces, and propose to begin with the lovely
valley of the Ahr.   As it is my intention to describe
the rivers of this district, with their capabilities for
affording sport, and the best places to go to, confining
myself simply to those that afford really good or fair
fishing, let me commence with certain conditions to

which every Englishman must make up his mind, if he is not acquainted with the language, and if he has had no experience of Germany and Germans. First, that he will have to pay for what he gets, not so extravagantly as in England, but more than he ought; and, secondly, that in many of the places I am about to describe neither French nor English is spoken; furthermore, that in many parts of Germany where formerly fishing was to be had to any amount, the people have found out its value, and charge accordingly. Nevertheless, I say that trout and grayling fishing is within reach of very many in this country who could not possibly afford it in England.

Having, then, arrived at Cologne—which, by the way, can be reached in a cheaper way, by booking yourself first-class *only as far as* Dover, paying for the steamer to Calais or Ostend on board, and then travelling second-class the remainder of the distance, taking care to get your luggage looked at as soon as possible on arrival at Calais, or the *through* carriages may be all taken up, and you will have to change half a dozen times. Having arrived at Cologne you book yourself to Bonn, or Remagen, by rail. I prefer the latter, as by driving up the valley of the Ahr you see the most magnificent scenery. Arrived at Remagen, go to the Hotel Furstenberg, where Otto Carraciola, the landlord, if he is still alive, will give you a good bottle of wine—Mem. Ask for Marcobrunner (white), or Walporzheimer (red)—and from thence take a carriage and pair to Altenahr. At Altenahr there are two hotels, a daily post, and newspapers. I can strongly recommend this as a first-rate head-quarters, for from it you can make excursions to no less than five or six rivers, besides the streams and brooks, which I am about to describe; the landlord boards and lodges you at so much per diem, according to agreement, and the fishing is, I believe, still free. Having, therefore, landed my readers at my starting point, I shall now endeavour to describe a few of the rivers and brooks that intersect the Rhenish provinces like a network, commencing with the lovely and romantic stream of

The Ahr.

The river Ahr is, perhaps, one of the most favoured of rivers in Rhenish Prussia, for it flows throughout its course along a valley never at any time more than half a mile in breadth, from whose edges rise a most precipitous range of slaty mountains. Following the course of the winding river, the sides of these mountains, as far as Dumpenfeld, are clothed with vineyards, which produce the Ahr wine, and the famous Walporzheimer, or red wine, of the district. The scenery is truly rugged and imposing, and, setting aside the fishing, the beautiful and magnificent panorama is alone worth seeing. The river, flows

5

over a rocky, gravelly bed, and is one continued stream, affording fishing every foot of the way, there being scarcely any flats whatever, but a continuation of streams and waterfalls. In the early part of the year—in April and May—the river is of a considerable size; but as the summer advances it recedes, and becomes much smaller, though still as large as the Wandle (to take an English instance), and in places larger.

The Ahr rises in a wine cellar near Blankenheim, and, after a tortuous course of some thirty miles, empties itself into the Rhine at Remagen. The river contains trout, grayling, chub, dace, gudgeon, stone-loach, and minnows. Of the first-mentioned—viz. trout—some fifteen years ago it was an easy matter to fill one's basket with them, varying from a quarter of a pound up to three pounds weight; but since the railway has been opened to Remagen, the constant request for trout by the various visitors to Altenahr, both German and English, has caused a considerable diminution of these fish; for the natives are not only up to burning the water, which they often resort to, but they also go out with pouch nets, so that between them and the coarse fish who eat their spawn the poor trout have a bad time of it. Notwithstanding this, a good basket of fish can easily be killed, though not of such a size as formerly, whilst a three-pound trout is a *rara avis*. If, however, the trout get a bad time of it, the grayling do not thus suffer, for, fortunately, foreigners do not appreciate this beautiful fish, and this kind of fishing is consequently very good. For my part, I would almost as soon have a good day's grayling--fishing as trout-fishing, especially in the Ahr, where they run to a good size. As to chub, they are a perfect nuisance, and here any Thames chub-fisher would go frantic with delight, as you may take them four or five pounds in weight. This river in the early part of the year is subject to frequent floods, which clear off as soon as they come, twelve hours generally making the river fishable.

So much for the Ahr, its inhabitants and characteristics. I now propose mentioning the best portions of the river to fish, how to get at them, and the best flies for various times of the year. I intend to be somewhat particular, as a day is very often lost by not knowing the water, and hours are wasted upon places where a passing cast or two would have proved sufficient.

Before proceeding with my description of the river Ahr, let me, for the benefit of my readers, state what are a few necessary adjuncts to the kit of anyone wishing to fish any of the streams which I am about to describe.

A single-handed rod will command any stream to be fished in this country; but I must confess that I lean to a double-handed one, from the advantage it

5 *

gives you to keep out of sight, fish far, and keeps
the line away from teazles, &c., on the bank. I would
have, therefore, a good general two-handed rod, of
fourteen feet in length, and a single-handed rod for
brook-fishing. A landing-net is absolutely necessary;
and, above all, wading stockings—many a light basket
should I have had had it not been for them. Don't
forget to bring your own soap, tobacco, and, if you are
a tea-drinker, your own tea. Let me also add to this
list a gridiron, on which you may sometimes cook
yourself a chop—which will be no slight delicacy,
believe me. Also some sort of contrivance for
catching minnows is necessary; and a quantity of
coarse gut and flies, to give away to the natives, often
get you a good day's fishing.

The river Ahr rises, as I stated above, in a wine cellar
near Blankenheim, some sixteen miles from Altenahr,
which latter is decidedly the best station as head-
quarters on the river. I divide the river into eight
parts, any of which is ample and more than sufficient
for a good hard day's fishing. The first beat is from
Aremberg to the village of Schuld. No. 2, from
Schuld to Dumpenfeld; in this portion there is
nothing but a mountain track, but at Dumpenfeld
you get the high road, which is excellent. At Dumpenfeld there is also a delightful brook running to
Adenau, of which more hereafter. No. 3 is from
Dumpenfeld to Brück. No. 4, from Brück to

Putzfeld. No. 5, from Putzfeld to Altenahr. No. 6, from Altenahr to Meyschloss. No. 7, from Mey-schloss to Ahrweiler; and No. 8, from Ahrweiler to Sinzig. Of these I prefer Nos. 8, 2, and 6, especially the last for grayling; but the upper waters of the Ahr are the best for trout.

The fishing from Ahrweiler to Sinzig is very mode-rate, and in some cases not worth going to. The best flies for the Ahr are the March brown in spring for trout, with the iron-blue dun; whilst for grayling the very best flies are the following: No. 1, orange body, ribbed with peacock harl with a cock-y-bondhu hackle at the shoulder, dressed as to size according to suit the water. No. 2, peacock body, gray hackle at shoul-der, and a red sprig of macaw for tail. No. 3, a dirty yellowish body, with a light dun hackle; the duns dark, yellow, and orange, also do well. Above all, let every man bring a good stock of red spinners, large and small, which are decidedly the best general fly. The months of May and part of June are the best on this river, and it is absolutely useless to go there before, as the river is full of thick, greenish-coloured water, and the fish do not take at all. Some heavy trout may be taken under the falls with a minnow, and the worm is very effective in warm months.

My readers must not suppose that fish are easily taken here; far from it. It requires a good fisherman and fine tackle to be successful; but, at any rate, there

are plenty of them. An average day's sport on the
Ahr ought to yield from two to three brace of trout
and from five to six brace of grayling. There are some
days, however, when a much larger basket can be
taken. I remember fishing the Ahr many years ago,
when I was a boy learning to speak German, and it
was no uncommon thing for me to fill my basket with
trout, some of them 3 lb. weight; of course of these
there were only a few. But I have taken as many as
seventy-five trout out of the Ahr in one day, commencing at half-past seven in the morning and fishing till
eight at night, between Schuld and Altenahr. This,
however, is a retrospect. The stream is excessively
clear, and the fish being continually disturbed are consequently very shy and require a deal of catching. The
mill-fall, just above Altenahr, holds some good trout;
as also the stream below it. There is a famous grayling
stream opposite Altenburg, the next village above
Altenahr; and the fall between Altenburg and Kreizberg may be fished with success. Do not pause to fish
any more water about Kreizberg, but proceed at once
beyond the village, and fish the first heavy stream
below the next fall; missing the next flat, fish the
streams under the church at Putzfeld, and if you are
anything of a hand I shall warrant me by this time
you have got a fair basket. Trout are in first-rate
condition in the Ahr after the 1st of April, although
they do not rise by any means freely; yet the

minnow will do some mischief. I have found a
March brown, tied in the following way, very effective: Tail, two strands of a dark woodcock hackle,
body a mixture of brown mohair, yellow, and a little
hare's ear, woodcock wings, and legs a dark woodcock hackle ; the whole tied with copper-coloured silk.

The Prussian laws relative to the renting and management of fisheries have of late undergone a very great
change. Some few years ago they were placed upon
exactly the same basis as the regulations respecting
shootings, but for some unaccountable reason they
have been altered. At present the law stands thus:
The fishings are put up to public auction every nine
years, and the highest bidder becomes the proprietor ;
but everyone who possesses *two inches* of ground on
the river can object to such rental, this objection
being valid, and should the river be taken or rented in
the face of such objection, the objector has a right to
angle over the lessee's water to the extent of such water
as is comprised in the limits of his parish. Furthermore, the lessee of such a piece of water has the right
to avail himself of any means he may think fit, to
assist him in catching the fish on such a piece of
water. And, lastly, fish prosecutions are rare, and
never end in anything but smoke. The consequence
is that the fish lead a bad time of it in those localities
where fish are appreciated, and where the taking of
them is a question of £. s. d. ; but I am happy to say

that there are still places, and many of them, where the angler need fear no hindrance, and where perhaps he is the only one who ever robs the water of their finny denizens. As to an Englishman getting justice here, that is entirely out of the question; and as a guide to my readers of the best course to pursue, I will relate what happened to me upon one occasion whilst fishing in a water that was unlet, and over which consequently every householder in the parish had a right of fishing.

In every village in Rhenish Prussia there is an individual appointed by Government to regulate its civil and criminal affairs, under the supervision of the chief magistrate of the district. This august personage is called a burgomaster. These burgomasters were formerly (in the good old times) appointed or chosen from amongst the oldest and most respected inhabitants of the town or village; but by a new law they are now appointed from a civil staff by the Government. In nine cases out of ten they are petty tyrants, who dearly love to show their consequence and authority, especially if they think they can do so without being called over the coals.

Now, it so happened that I was desirous of fishing a tributary of the Kesseling brook, and in an unguarded moment I forgot to stick to my usual method in such cases — namely, that of putting some silver groschen in my pocket—but went to the burgomaster of the district, stated my case, and begged his influence to obtain for me permission to fish.

"Oh," said he, " here is my card; this is quite sufficient; you can do anything you please, or go where you like with it."

Accordingly I started (having some eight miles to go) early in the morning, and having arrived at my destination I commenced operations. Of trout there were plenty the length of my finger, which rose eagerly at anything you liked to throw them; but fish of any size or condition there were none. I had got seven or eight little wretches in my creel when two German yokels accosted me, without the usual preface of "Guten tag" (good day), by saying that if I threw my line upon the water again they would take me into custody.

Now, it so happened that upon this particular day I felt that I had a liver, and consequently I was anything but amiably disposed; so, in an equally rough way, and, to their astonishment, in "platt Deutsch," or low German, I told them to go to the d—l, as I had leave from the burgomaster, and should fish as much as I pleased. They informed me that the burgomaster had nothing to do with it, that the fishing was not let, and that consequently each individual in the village had a right to fish and prevent strangers from so doing. I told them I didn't care twopence for them or their fishing, but that I should go on and do as I pleased.

They shortly went away, and I was beginning to congratulate myself upon my having got rid of them, when I saw another individual, in company with the two former ones, approaching me. They came to within twenty yards, and stood watching me. At this moment I caught a wretched trout the length of my thumb. No sooner did they see this than the new arrival, without a " with your leave " or " by your leave," made a rush at me and tried to take my rod away. Not being particularly partial to such liberties, I landed him quietly in the middle of the brook, upon which the other two made a rush at me, for which I was fortunately prepared. Having a spike at the butt of my rod, I sent it into the first fellow's stomach, and I let the other have a right-hander between the eyes, which astonished him immensely.

By this time my friend in the brook scrambled out, holding his right arm in the air for my inspection, and drawing my attention to a brass badge bearing the arms of Prussia upon it, and at the same time telling me he was a " patrol," and that I had struck him and must take the consequences. Now, knowing as I do the very stringent rules about striking any Prussian official, I thought it better to surrender my rod, at the same time requesting that he would accompany me to the burgomaster.

Accordingly, escorted by five individuals, not one of them reaching higher than my shoulder, I started off to the residence of this all-powerful official. Now it so happened that this was placed at a good three miles' distance from the place where I had met the "patrol," and it being a sweltering hot day, I determined to give my friends a treat for spoiling my day's fishing. Knowing perfectly well that they would never permit me to get there first and tell my story, I accordingly laid down to my work with a will, and being gifted with good long legs, I soon distanced my followers. From a walk they got into a jog-trot, and when we arrived at our destination I never saw a more miserable-looking lot of wretches.

Fortunately for me I speak German, and "platt Deutsch," or Low German also, otherwise the astounding lies which the patrol told would, no doubt, have found credence with the burgomaster. However, I plainly told him the case, and that if I did not at once get back my rod I should write immediately to Berlin, and, after a good deal of haggling I got it back; but had I been unused to Germans or unable to speak the language, I should have lost my rod, and in all probability been fined into the bargain.

The great secret is a five-groschen piece (6d.) Go to the head man of the village, show him your rod, and present him with the above-named sum, and no one will interfere with you; but put not your trust in burgomasters, and, above all, do not strike a Prussian official.

I mentioned eight different beats on the Ahr, which said beats comprise the main body of the river; but if the angler wants to get really good trout-fishing he must ascend to its head waters, which he can do by taking the post from Altenahr in the evening and going to Adenau. Arrived at Adenau, he must rise at six in the morning, and, having ordered a trap, drive to a place called Nöhn, about seven miles from Adenau. Here he will find a small Gasthaus, or inn, where the goodness of the fishing will make up for the roughness of his fare and the hardness of his bed. This stream is called the Ahrbach, and a truly delightful one it is, holding heavy trout, no coarse fish, and extending for some miles. It is one of those streams which form the head waters of the Ahr, and of which I now propose to give a description.

The tributaries that form the head waters of the Ahr are three in number—viz., the Ahrbach, the Blankenheim Brook, and the Reer. The Ahrbach rises in the hills above Nöhn, some two hours' drive from Adenau, the principal town in this locality, and after a run of some six or seven miles it meets the Blankenheim Brook at Ahrdorf; these two joined together make the first waters of the river Ahr. A little way lower down the Reer increases the volume by discharging its waters into the Ahr at Nüsch, and the river Ahr then flows of an uniform size until it falls into the Rhine. To reach any of these streams from

Altenahr, it is necessary the evening before you intend
fishing to take the post as far as Adenau, sleep at the
hotel of the Half Moon, and charter a trap from there
to Nöhn for the Ahrbach, to Wirft for the Reer, and
to Ahrdorf for the Blankenheim Brook. I am now
mentioning the best places to commence fishing at in
each of these streams. You can then return to
Adenau for the night. Such a journey can be easily
done by a single person for 30s. English, including
carriage fare, remaining if you like in Adenau for two
days.

For undeniably good trout-fishing I do not think I
ever saw any stream I liked better than the Ahrbach.
It is not so much for the number or size of its trout
as for their beautiful appearance, excessive gameness,
and condition. Its waters are not wide, but in places
the sharp streams run into immensely deep holes, which
the natives are unable to net, and consequently
this stream is always full of trout. On a good day
you ought to kill twenty brace, and I will warrant the
average to be $\frac{1}{2}$ lb. I was there a short time ago and
had only time to remain on its seductive banks for two
hours. The flies I used was the furnace fly, the hare's
ear dun, and the Grannom, or greentail. I killed 17
trout, three of which weighed together $4\frac{1}{4}$ lb., or
averaging a little over $1\frac{1}{4}$ lb. each; they were the
gamest fish I have taken for some time, and reminded
me of the Loddon trout at Basingstoke more than any-

thing. The total weight was 12½ lb., and I had nothing under ½ lb.

At Nöhn ten groschen (one shilling) will readily get you leave, and you will then require to ask permission at the first mill you come to, which will be readily granted. The stream is in prime fishing order in April and May, but the water becomes so small later in the season that the trout shift down into the Ahr. This may be said, too, of the Blankenheim Brook, which rises in a cellar in Blankenheim, and holds, like its twin sister the Ahrbach, good fish and strong. The same I may also add of the Reer, though the Reer is inferior, in my opinion, to the other two. Still trout of 2 lb. to 3 lb. have been taken in it. The landlord of the Half Moon at Adenau will smooth the way as to permission to fish.

I must strongly recommend anyone stopping at Altenahr to take this trip, as the fishing in April and May is very good. I have taken in one day 25 lb. weight of trout out of the Reer with the furnace fly. There is no necessity to know the water, or for me to explain, as every stream you come to is as good as its fellow, and holds any number of fish. But you must fish fine, and make up your mind to lose a few flies, as the banks are in many places choked with alder bushes. Wading, as I said before, is indispensable; indeed, I never could understand how a man who really enjoyed fishing could get on without wading. I do not say it is necessary to paddle all over the stream, muddying its waters and disturbing the fish—no fisherman or sportsman would be guilty of such a thing—but wading is an immense advantage if judiciously made use of.

There is one great disadvantage, however, in fishing these three streams—viz., the necessity of going to and returning from Adenau every morning and evening, as there is really no inn or hotel where an Englishman would care to pass the night. This, however, is amply repaid by the lovely scenery one passes through on the way to the fishing.

The Lanterat, or chief magistrate at Adenau, is excessively polite to strangers, and always willing to further their wishes as far as lays in his power. In addition to this, there are two places in the neighbourhood of Adenau which the sight-seer should visit. One is the magnificent ruin of Nurburg, and the other is the Höh Ach or the highest point in the Rhenish provinces. It is 2,400 feet above the level of the sea, and from its summit, which is easily reached by a carriage road, can be seen the seven hills on the Rhine, Cologne, the Westphalian hills, and the vast panorama of the Rhine as it winds its tortuous course to Coblenz. When you return from Adenau you can fish the Adenau Brook, commencing about two miles below Adenau. It is but " a bit burnie," but in spring it holds some good trout.

Some persons dislike being encumbered with net and basket whilst fishing; should that be the case, there are plenty of boys who will engage to go out daily from Altenahr for five or six groschen per diem (from 6d. to 7½d.) They are excessively handy with a landing net, and very careful not to show themselves or tread upon or damage your tackle; they also take a great interest in fishing, and get as excited over a good fish as one does oneself.

Very erroneous reports get into circulation through channels such as the one I am about to describe, respecting continental streams and the capabilities they afford of giving the angler sport.

The reports I allude to are such as these. One day, whilst fishing the Ahr, I met a countryman industriously flogging the river to no purpose. I offered my assistance, but was rudely repulsed, with the assertion that he did not require instruction, and was fully able to take care of himself. In the evening he paid me a visit, having somewhat altered his mind, no doubt having heard from the natives of some of my successes. I was, however, notwithstanding his brusqueness in the morning, perfectly willing to assist him, and told him if he liked to accompany me I would take him to the best part of the river. He complained further that he could not imagine that there were any trout in the stream, or else he would have been *sure* to take some.

He then asked me to show him my flies, which I did, telling him that the fish were by no means easy to take, and very capricious, not taking the same fly each day or hour. Having pumped me and obtained all the news he could get, together with half a dozen flies, he left me, and a little later sent a note saying he could not accompany me on the morrow. I was not sorry for this, but was somewhat surprised on the following morning to see my friend thrashing the river on the very part I had told him I intended fishing. However, I went farther up, had a good day's sport, and on my return in the evening, I found him awaiting my arrival.

"Well," he cried, "there was no excuse to-day, water in splendid order, wind and weather first-rate, but I could not stir or take a fish. Of course you did nothing."

Now it happened, for the reputation of this stream, that I had in my creel seventeen trout, one of them 2 lb. in weight, two of 1 lb., and the others averaging $\frac{1}{2}$ lb. I was, however, so disgusted with this individual that I parted company. Had I not chanced to be on the spot, no doubt this person—who knew as much about trout-fishing as hat-making, probably more of the latter —would have told everyone that trout-fishing in the Ahr was a myth.

The river Kyll is another beautiful stream of the Rhine provinces which is well worth the angler's atten-

tion, particularly its upper waters. In size it re-
sembles the Nette, but for some reason or another,
which lies most probably in the soil or strata it
flows through, its fish are neither so game nor so good
as those taken in either the Nette or Ahr. It is,
however, a lovely stream, flowing through a wild
and picturesque country. The largest fish I captured
weighed 1¾ lb.; the average may be put down at ¼ lb.

This stream is a late one, the fish being in order no
earlier than the 1st May. The flies on this river are
much the same as I before mentioned, with the exception that the red fly and alder are thicker on it
than on most continental streams. The last day I
fished it I used the blue dun and furnace in the
morning, with the soldier palmer and sandfly in the
afternoon. The sandfly I used was dressed buzz, with
the red covert feather of the landrail's wing, body from
the fur on the hare's poll, with a tinge of greenish
mohair through it, and ribbed with orange silk.

The Kyll rises in the Eifel above Stadtkyll, and, after
a course of some forty miles, falls into the Mosel some
miles above Coblenz. The best stations for fishing
this stream are Stadtkyll, Hillesheim, and Gerolstein.
There are also a few little brooks in the neighbourhood of Hillesheim that can give a good day's sport
when the water will allow it.

The minnow is a killing bait in the Kyll, which is
peculiarly adapted to this mode of fishing from its

continuous streamy nature, and many waterfalls and cascades.

Below the places I have mentioned the water is infested with coarse fish, and I am sorry to say a good many pike out of the Mosel, so that to the flyfisher these places are almost useless, though a " big one " is now and then to be met with. At all the places I have mentioned capital accommodation can be procured, and they can be reached either from Coblenz, or Adenau, *viâ* Remagen on the Rhine.

The Sieg is a river-stream traversing a very considerable portion of Westphalia. It rises in the hills near Paddeborn and falls into the Rhine at Siegburg. Salmon are to be met with in the lower portions of the Sieg, though they are scarce and won't look at a fly; you have a chance with a minnow, but it is a poor one. The best part of this river is about Siegen, as far as Olpe on the west, and about fifteen miles above Siegen; the other portions swarm with chub and dace, but at the places I have mentioned fair trout-fishing can be got. In Olpe there are two good hotels; this place can be reached by rail from Cologne; the rail goes on to Siegen, where too, there is ample accommodation. There are several mill-dams in the neighbourhood of Olpe which contain heavy trout, but you must use the minnow, as the fly is useless. The Sieg has many tributaries, which all contain trout in more or less quantities.

6 *

The river Nette is another beautiful stream form-
ing one of the many tributaries of the Rhine, and
is easy of access to the angler from Altenahr, Ander-
nach, or Coblenz; for you can leave Altenahr at
seven in the morning, and be fishing in the Nette at
11 A.M. Should the angler contemplate a stay upon its
banks, the town of Mayen furnishes a capital lodging,
with good and convenient hotels. The Nette is about
the same size as the Ahr; it contains trout, grayling,
chub, dace, roach, gudgeon, minnows, and eels in
various quantities. Its upper waters— viz. from Mayen
to Langenfeld—are the best, as indeed, are all the
waters of these streams; but fair fishing is to be had
below Mayen, especially below Trimbs. Its head
waters are formed by a number of small brooks, which
rise in the hills between Virnebourgh and Langenfeld,
and, uniting just above Gurrenberg, form the Nette
proper.

The great quantity of white fish to be found,
together with the usual poaching propensities of the
inhabitants, have reduced the trout to a very small
amount in comparison to former years; yet there
is still great inducement to visit its banks, and many
a good fish is still sporting in its limpid waters. Like
the Ahr it is subject to frequent floods, which as soon
clear off, and in a few hours the water is in prime
fishing order. The early months of spring, such as
April and May, are ever the best for the flyfisher, as

the water is then too cold to admit of the natives
fishing it by night with torches, or by day with pout-
nets. The grayling run larger here, but in fewer
numbers than in the Ahr, although the trout are not
of such fine quality.

Permission to fish is to be obtained in the usual
way by application to the principal man of the nearest
village and the dispensing of a few silver groschen.
But the angler is far less likely to meet with interrup-
tion, as this part of the country is not nearly so largely
populated, nor are there so many villages upon the
river's bank.

As a guide to my readers I will relate my last
excursion from Altenahr to the Nette, with its net
results, if I may be allowed the atrocious pun.

The month was the blooming one of May—somewhat colder that year than one likes to see, but nevertheless propitious so far as sport is concerned. We
summoned our trusty follower to consult upon the
importance of a day on the Nette before the fish
should have been so disturbed as to make them sulky
and unlikely to rise freely at the fly. Our attendant
merits description, as he is one of those with whom
the Englishman who needs an attendant will be
brought into contact. I am aware that one like him
whose services I secured is not always to be got,
but there are many, though not quite so handy as he
was, just as enthusiastic and as easily taught.

In good old England there is a certain class of
the labouring poor amongst whom one always looks
for the fishing celebrity of the village. This is generally either the blacksmith, the shoemaker, or the
miller. It is easy to understand that the miller's
continual residence or occupation on the river's bank
naturally induces him to take to angling; but why the
other two should, in nine cases out of ten, be adepts in
the gentle art, is a question I must leave to wiser
heads to discover. Be that as it may, each country
has its peculiarity, and in Germany (or at least in the
Rhine provinces) butchers are the piscatorial cele-
brities.

Franz Grimegor, fleischer, or flesher, or butcher,
was the name of my *ci-devant* attendant. I recollect
thinking that " fleischer " was his surname at first,
and continually called him this until his risible facul-
ties could withstand my absurd mistake no longer; on
its discovery, I think I laughed as much as he did.
Nevertheless, Franz was an excellent attendant, from
his habits of catching fish with worm, net, and hand.
He knew what he was about; he was first-rate with
the landing-net ; and never tired from morning to night.
I paid him 6d. per diem, treated him to occasional
glasses of wine and cigars, and could not tire him. He
would carry as much fish as I could catch, and all my
traps and waterproofs from morning to night, only
murmuring when there was no sport. He could

already throw and tie a fly in no mean way for a no-
vice. He stood but 5ft. 5½in., and was my factotum.
Now, reader, you have a somewhat hasty description
of a very usual sort of man to be met with in the wilds,
and if I add that he had an imperturbable temper, I
have said enough.

Well, Franz and I agreed that some flies must be at
once tied, and that the next morning must see us
across the mountains to Langenfeld. Accordingly I
set to work, and a dozen insects of various kinds soon
graced my little table. Next morning, in the comfortable carriage of the host of the Hotel Gaspari and
with his willing boy, at half-past 5 A.M. we left
Altenahr, and after a most lovely drive of about two
hours and a half arrived at the little village of
Langenfeld. The river at this point is very much
wooded on both sides, and, unless there has been
plenty of rain, is likely to present but little chance of
success, and, with the exception of a small trickling
rill, we found it on this occasion almost dry. Here
was a nice position! However, fish I must and
would. So I despatched a boy to tell the man to go
home with the carriage, and that I would pursue the
course of the river until I found it fishable, and
return the next evening. Accordingly off I trudged,
Franz beguiling the way by telling me that the chapel
which I saw opposite was the chapel of St. Jost,
where a wonderful miracle had been performed,

inasmuch as a young girl who had lost the use of one of her legs from paralysis, or some such malady, had been cured by visiting this sacred place. He also, with many lamentations, told me how that he on a former occasion, having suffered dreadfully from rheumatism, had offered alms and oblations without propitiating his saintship, or any good accruing to him from his attentions and donations.

I saw a good many " hazel hühner " in the woods, and a hare or two ; and after a lovely walk of about one hour and a half, I found myself at a spot where two burns increased the water sufficiently to permit of my fishing.

The yellow dun and blue dun were out thick, as also the alder and black gnat, and with these four flies I took eight brace of fish, weighing $7\frac{1}{4}$ lb., and two fish, one of 2 lb. and one $1\frac{1}{4}$ lb. The best part of the water is decidedly about four miles from Mayen, and on second thoughts I should recommend anyone wishing to fish the Nette to go to this place; for from this you can go to the Laacher See, a very large sheet of water containing pike, perch, bream, lake trout, and eels. You are also close to the Rhine and at easy distance from Coblentz.

The partridge hackle and a fly dressed as follows are favourites on the Nette: Hook No. 9 or 10; body, white floss silk ribbed with yellow; legs, a honey dun hackle; wings, the molted feather from a woodcock's wing; tail, two strands of a grizzled hackle. There are a great many of these flies on the water in May, and I have taken a good many fish with it.

Before quitting the Ahr and its tributaries let me once more caution my readers against expecting any trout-fishing *below* Altenahr. The trout-fishing gradually improves the higher you go above it, and on some spots he must indeed be a muff who cannot kill five or six brace of trout. On the other hand, grayling are more plentiful below Altenahr than above, and capital sport they afford.

There is a fly which the trout are very fond of on this river in the month of April, and which I have never seen on our streams at home. I imitate it in the following manner: Hook No. 6 Kendal bend; tail, two fibres from the feather of a mallard, inclined to a reddish brown; body, long and thin, dark maroon floss silk ribbed with yellow silk, and a small tip of red floss silk at the tail; legs a honey dun hackle; wings, two gray hackles, inclined to brown, dressed upright. Fish it on windy days, when it is blowing a hurricane. It only lasts for a month, and I do not know its name.

A DAY AMONGST THE PIKE.

————◆————

THERE is a certain satisfaction in the reflection that although we are treading the path of life's declining years, nothing can rob us of the glory of bygone achievements by flood or field. How pleasant to dream over the old battles, made dear to our memories by their associations, and marked in the diary of our mind as red-letter days. Although some few years have gone by, that which I am about to relate seems as green in my memory as if it had happened yesterday, and although my companion and I are not quite so young and active as we used to be, still my pulse beats a throb quicker as I remember the incidents I am about to relate. It was a week before Christmas ; the weather for once had been seasonable, cold, clear, and frosty, with a sprinkle of snow—

weather that cuts the weed down and enables the lover of pike-fishing to get at the sacred haunts of the fish. "If I could only get leave for a day at ——," I mentally pondered, "what sport I should have. I'll write and ask." I did so, and one fine morning I got the reply—my request was granted. That answer came at breakfast. I couldn't eat any, I was in a perfect fever of excitement, and the first thing that occurred to me was, Who can I ask to go with me? for I am a gregarious animal, and to enjoy anything alone is to me an impossibility. I did not think very long, and before ten minutes were over, I had despatched a note to my old friend and companion on many a river's side, whose name is familar as a household word in every angler's mouth, and I added a P.S.: "You must bring the bait, and, mind, some large dace, for we shall have to battle with big ones."

The day I fixed upon was Christmas Eve, and the overhauling of my tackle was a matter which occupied every spare moment in the interim. The water we were going to fish is now, I believe, destitute of such a thing as a pike, and has, since the death of the late noble owner, been turned entirely into a trout river, with what success I know not. At the time I am speaking of, report said that it contained fish of enormous size, but, somehow, no one seemed to be able to catch them. All the more exciting, and my dreams were filled with visions of broken top joints, a catch in the reel, ugly roots of trees, bad hooks, and the *hoc genus omne* of miseries that make up the fisherman's nightmare.

At length the day arrived, and the 7 A.M. train found me at Waterloo to pick up my friend at Clapham Junction. It was dark and very frosty; a frost, just enough to cut the weed down, and perhaps—I shuddered at the thought—put a thin cake of ice on the water. Well, no matter, I must go, and trust to that providence which always stands true to the enthusiast; and, as the train glided out of the station, my thoughts were somewhat on this wise :—

"Wonder if he's got some good dace? Who's going to carry the bait-cans down to the water? Will there be a boat, or can we command the water from the bank? Shall we have to walk from the station, or can we get a fly? What sort of a chap will the keeper be?"

And by this time the train was coming into Clapham Junction, my head was out of the window a long time before the train came to a standstill, and I had spotted those bait-cans long before I saw anything else; and there, too, was the jolly, cheery, good-humoured face, with a bundle of rods in one hand, and a basket in the other. I shouted, he shouted, we both shouted; for, sport or no sport, we were going fishing together. Did we have a dram and light a pipe? Did we "hit the ceiling"? as they say in America. Might as well ask one as the other. And then those bait-cans were an awful nuisance; the water slopped, and slopped, until the bottom of the carriage was a perfect deluge, and the fish half dead. At last we arrived at the small station where we were to alight. It was not an inviting station, but—yes, there was a fly. I hailed that man in no very measured tones, my friend hailed him too, and, as I saw another head looking out of another window, I stuck a half-crown in my eye. He saw it, and we caught that fly.

"How far is it to——?" was, of course, the first question. "About a mile and a half, Sir"; and the traps were bundled in, taking care to change the water in the bait-cans at a pond before getting under way. The wind had risen a little, and as it rustled amongst the tops of the firs close by, it set the signboard creaking of the little inn, reminding us that there was a haven of refreshment. We looked at one another, and, with that unanimous sentiment which inspires all good fishermen, we refused to take a shingle off the roof of that inn, so we went into the —— Arms. Dear old place! the kitchen was the bar, and a roaring fire of fir logs burning in the capacious fire-place. The landlord had gone to his work; it was but a small old-fashioned country inn, where as yet the fable of the "Three Acres and a Cow" had not been whispered—and the landlady suggested something hot, the while dangling on her finger what looked to me like a tin funnel of peculiar shape. That funnel was put into

the embers, and in a short time, I had a glass of the
most perfect elixir, frothy, creaming, and yellow, that I
had ever tasted—then we started.

Now, between my friend and myself there was no
jealousy. To catch fish was what we wanted, and
whether he did it or I was a matter of small considera-
tion; so there was no racing to put rods together, to
get first to the water, or anything of that sort. But
it was, "Are you all right, old man? Can I help
you? I think I've got a better trace than that, will
you have it?" &c. Now, be it remembered, neither
he nor I had ever seen this glorious bit of water; next,
there was no keeper to meet us, and so we had to trust
to our own experience. We started in the open water
opposite the house, and commenced spinning with a
small dace on a flight of nine hooks and a flying
triangle from the mouth. We were cold, and the
exercise warmed us; it also made our backs ache,
especially as, after fishing for about three-quarters of
an hour, a miserable little fish of two pounds was all
that rewarded our efforts.

We sat down, lit a pipe, and looked at one another.
There was a something about that look which is
entirely indescribable. There was a word that fluttered to our lips that I shall refrain from writing, but
you know what it was. We wayed down the bank
of the river until we came to an island. Beyond this
island and to the right of it there was a sort of lake or

back-water formed by a sluice-gate and dam from the
river proper. Upon this piece of water, about three
to four acres in extent, rode a miniature yacht, a
cutter, naturally laid up for the winter, the ballast out
of her, and consequently very light; at her best she
could not have held more than two people. My friend
was tired, I think a little disgusted, because his
answers to me were somewhat abbreviated, and so I
let him make for that little yacht without venturing a
remark, whilst I sat down to watch him from the
opposite bank. I saw him take off his trace and put
live-bait tackle on; I saw him climb into that little
yacht, and with great difficulty seat himself, because
she was very light, and I had fiendish hopes that she
would capsize. But she did not. I watched him as
he swung that great red float out, and then I took a
turn on my side, spinning. I was not very happy,
because I thought the whole thing a fizzle, and so I
commenced admiring how beautifully my bait span;
no wobble; how sweetly the line went out through
those large rings; and, though it was blowing, never
a kink; until just as I was indolently taking in the
last few feet, a flash of silver shot across the water, and
I was into a good fish—at the same moment my friend
landed a good 6-lb. fish from his crazy craft, and from
then the sport was fast and furious.

At 3 o'clock we had forty-one fish averaging 5 lbs.
on the bank, and were both fairly tired out—he

live-baiting, I spinning. Some of the fish weighed 10 lbs., short, thick, well-fed fish; such an array I have never seen, nor, indeed, had anyone there. Please to remember, reader, that these fish were caught live-baiting with snap-tackle and spinning; for I hold in the utmost contempt the man who fishes with a gorge-bait. To him large or small fish are equal sport, if you can use such an expression for that which, to my mind, is nothing more nor less than poaching. But with snap-tackle or a spinning flight a small fish can be returned to the water, but with a gorge it is impossible to do anything else than destroy the fish after it has pouched the bait.

We were fairly exhausted, and the short day was drawing to a close, when I proposed that we should put on two large dace on snap-tackle and live-bait the neck of water just above the sluice, he from the island above described, and I from the opposite bank. I said, "Perhaps we shall catch one of the big ones." No sooner said than done. The spot I chose was an opening made under some willows; and I am free to confess I did not pay much attention to the surroundings, or I should have hesitated. My friend flung haphazard out immediately opposite me. The dace I had on must have been close upon 1 lb., and the large red float could scarcely control him, so lively was he. All of a sudden the red float stood still and hung up, I thought, and I was just going to move him when

I saw a white streak dash through the water and the red float disappear. Instinctively I struck. Horror! the top of my rod went into the willows above me; I had forgotten about those willows, and I muttered something as the winch whizzed out. At that moment I heard an exclamation from my friend. I looked up and saw him fighting a fish with his rod bent nearly double. I had no time to do more than look, as my fish occupied all my attention, and the willows did *not* help me. I said to my friend, "Land your fish and come and help me." He answered: "I can't; I've got all I can do." And there we were, hammer and tongs opposite one another for a good ten minutes. The result was he had to land his own fish and I landed mine. His weighed 19 lbs., and mine 22½ lbs. He had the female fish and I the male; and I feel sure my readers will take some interest in the above reminiscence of a magnificent day's sport when I tell them that my companion was the late Mr. Francis Francis.

THE PHILOSOPHY OF ANGLING.

I NEED hardly say that the art of angling is one whose praises have been oftentimes tunefully sung and written upon since the days of Izaak Walton, the great High Priest of Anglers. I therefore approach this subject with the painful conviction that I have, perhaps, nothing new to tell beyond what has been already so much better and more ably commented upon by others. And yet it has occurred to me that there is, perhaps, one phase connected with angling which has not been thought out in its entirety. I mean the relations which are established between man and man amongst various nations, civilized and savage, by the cultivation of the gentle art. It has been my pleasure and privilege to have fished in many countries of the Old and New world: in the Old world, the British Isles, France, Germany,

Russian Poland, Norway, Belgium, Austria, Italy, Switzerland, Iceland, and the sluggish rivers of central India ; in the New world, the glorious Canadian lakes and rivers, the lakes and rivers of New England, and the Northern States of America, whilst I have wet my line as far south as the lagoons and rivers of Florida. Anywhere and everywhere I have been struck by the influence which angling, as an occupation or an amusement, has upon the character of those engaged in its pursuit.

I take it that the individual who voted angling a cruel, stupid pastime, had not reasoned out the philosophy of the subject he thoughtlessly censured. I may be wrong, but to be an angler—there are many fishermen, but comparatively few anglers—a man must be of a nature thoroughly unselfish, an ardent admirer and student of God's handiwork, be it tree, flower, or insect, of an open-hearted and generous disposition, a keen observer, especially as regards atmospheric influences, and he must also be endowed with sufficient physical power, so that the pursuit of angling may not become a burden instead of a pleasant and instructive occupation. Now if a man possessing all these attributes can be called stupid or cruel, then I say that all of us who love the gentle art have wasted much time and must be ranked amongst the cruel and stupid. But this cannot be so. For if we refer back to the history of great

7 *

men, it will be found that many of them were more
or less anglers, and that the great criminals who
have worthily suffered for their misdeeds have never
known the gentle influence of the placidly flowing
river or the brawling brook—have never looked

Through Nature up to Nature's God.

Perhaps a brighter and better specimen of an
angler, who eminently possessed the qualities I have
named above, in addition to his wondrous art, could
not be found than my very dear friend and oft companion by the river-side, the late Mr. H. D. Rolfe
—God rest his memory! I daresay that many who
read these lines knew him. Many is the pleasant
expedition I have had with him. His was a truly
unselfish and beautiful nature; he was never known
to get up at day-break so as to be first on the
river's bank, or to hasten in front of a brother
angler so as to get the best of the water; his fly-book
or tackle-box was open to all, his flask and tobacco-
pouch at anyone's service; whilst his purse has often
supplied, with generous charity, the wants of the
needy or distressed. Could anyone call such a
nature cruel and stupid?

But I digress. I take it, then, that those who
enunciate such principles can never have studied the
subject of angling from a philosophical point of view,
and therefore we may dismiss them as narrow-minded

miserable fellow-creatures who have missed a portion
of their lives. Angling, as a pastime or an occupation, has its different effects on different natures. In
England, Scotland, Ireland and Wales it has caused
and does cause a bond of unity which no Bill in Parlia-
ment will ever disunite. The sturdy Englishman,
the calculating though generous Scotchman, the
warm-hearted wrong-headed Irishman, the impetuous
Welshman, all shake hands with one another by the
water's side. They all agree on the one subject
which forms a bond of pleasant unity about which
there is but one opinion, one voice, "love of the
gentle art," and to be in charity with all men.

In France our neighbours are not so happy as
we are, and the pursuit has a different effect upon
their excitable natures. The Seine is to Parisians
what the Thames is to Londoners—only mark the
difference :—

"In the report of the Seine Conservancy for the
year 1884, under the heading 'Animals found in the
Seine,' during the summer of that year, I find 3,929
dogs, 349 cats, 1,916 rats, 191 fowls, 130 rabbits, 23
pieces of meat, 8 geese, 3 turkeys, 2 wild boars,
2 sheep, 1 goat, 1 pig, one calf, one monkey, and
eight fishes." Of course the question arises whether
the fishes were drowned by accident, or whether they
died from natural causes. Personally, I am inclined
to think that they were bought alive by some prac-

tical angling wag at the fish-market, who threw
them in on purpose to beguile a friend, a disciple of
the rod, into the belief that the Seine was pisca-
torially occupied, and that these fishes died from
miasma, or perhaps old age. For during many years
that I have watched the quays in Paris, I have never
seen one live fish, however small, caught. And yet
these quays, on the 15th, were crowded early in the
morning, to celebrate the opening of the angling
season. There was joy depicted on every face of
these worthies of the rod—old and young—and their
joy is incomprehensible, seeing that it is doomed to
disappointment. I always used to meet the same faces
whenever I visited those quays; with some of them
I became familiar — nay, friendly. One among
them I assisted in deciphering Izaak Walton, and his
gratitude is lasting, at least in interest. He has
promised to invite me to a fish dinner of his own
catching. The promise was given three years ago,
but my legs have not found their way under his
mahogany yet; but I am certain that the smallest
gudgeon safely landed will be followed by a telegram that the feast is spread. He himself is impatient for a convivial meeting at his house, but he
has made a vow that I shall not cross his threshold
except to rejoice in the long-expected triumph. My
prospective host is a man of birth and breeding; he
has a very extensive knowledge of the literature of

his own country, he converses fluently and instructively on most subjects, but I have never dared to ask him outright if he has ever caught a fish. I know he would not tell me a falsehood—the truth might be too painful to reveal.

Are there many of these unsuccessful anglers in Paris? At a rough guess I should say close upon a thousand. Statistics reveal the presence of 12,000 anglers with the rod in France; but, judging from the aspect of the river's side for ten months in the year, and that no licence is required, this must be underrated, and out of the one thousand I should say at least four hundred have never felt the joy of landing ever so small a fish upon the bank. "Never mind the result, the excitement and emotions of the chase alone suffice," says my friend. This philosophy must be a true one, or else the angling records of France would not be so crowded with illustrious names.

The Curator of the Bibliothèque Nationale once told me that 50 per cent of his most valuable *personnel* were anglers with the rod. M. Messonier is an enthusiastic votary. M. Ambroise Thomas, the composer of the opera of *Mignon*, is supposed to find his most tuneful airs whilst watching his float. Rossini acknowledged to having found one of his magnificent trios whilst angling on the estate of Mr. Aguado. Alphonse Karr, Emile Augier, Jules San-

deau swell the list of French anglers. But the most
striking feature of the philosophy of the Parisian
angler is the persistency with which he will select a
spot and stick to it in spite of failure. Should he
by chance vacate it, there are a dozen successors
ready to take his place. His inopportune return
gives rise to comic scenes; for the inveterate French
angler, though peaceful enough whilst plying his
craft, is pugnacious.

A few years ago a friend of mine, an eminent
Parisian journalist, had the misfortune to institute a
comparison between the fly-fisher and the bottom fisher.
He opined that the former was more active, more
intelligent, more skilful, and consequently more prone
to resent a slight. A gentleman of the latter per-
suasion felt offended at this insinuation, and chal-
lenged him to single combat. They did not fight.

Again, while the Hôtel de la Monnaie was burning during the Commune, several anglers who had
helped to set it on fire returned to their peg by the
river-side, telling their companions to call them if
they were wanted. They expressed no joy at the
destruction they had wrought, but they eagerly en-
quired if anyone had caught a fish during their
absence.

As a rule the French angler, when engaged in his
favourite pursuit, is profoundly indifferent to surrounding events. During the first day of the July

revolution, Compigny, the well-known friend of Mdlle. Mars, and the head of a department at the Ministry of Public Education, remained peacefully seated beneath the Bridge of Arts plying his rod, while on both sides of the bridge the terrific struggle was going on, and over his head the artillery was thundering. M. Salvady, Minister of Public Instruction during the reign of Louis Philippe, reinstated a provincial professor whom he had dismissed because the latter had by the merest accident settled himself in his favourite spot under the bridge *de la Concorde.* "I should have yielded my position in the Ministry to my most persistent political adversary," he said, "in order to get rid of him." What becomes of these ardent votaries during the close time? Some fish, in spite of the law, but they do not use rods. They attach a line to their ankle and dangle it for hours beneath the surface of the stream. Among these is Barre, a *sociétaire* of the Comédie Française, a very eminent actor. Others go to Sceaux, where they fish upon a piece of private water for 50 centimes and a fee for their tackle. The water abounds in carp, but the administration makes the angler pay for every fish he catches. It provides a new emotion. The angler's pride prompts him to wish for good sport. His spirit of economy makes him furious at a bite. The other day I met five French anglers who had not heard of the Ex-

pulsion Bill, and when told of it they expressed their
sympathy with one member of the Orleans family
only, and that was because he was a good fisherman.

Now it is very evident that no British angler
was, or ever could be, influenced in such a manner
as our neighbours across the Channel, although the
bond of unity is strengthened, though in a different
manner, by the pursuit of the gentle art.

In Canada and North America the Indian or half-
breed looks with sorrow upon the often wanton takes
of the white man, who, with that inherent thirst for
sport so characteristic of the Anglo-Saxon, revels
in heavy baskets of salmon, trout, bass, &c. Is
it because the one is a sportsman, and the other
not ? By no means—the red man is the keenest
of sportsmen, it is almost his religion, but his
simple philosophy revolts from the inordinate destruction of those things which the Great Being has made,
he believes, for the subsistence of his red children;
whilst the Anglo-Saxon is only intent upon the
number and weight of his bag. The least vicious of
all the tribes, now swept away by the march of civiliza-
tion, were the Marragansetts, who inhabited the sea
coast of New England, and lived entirely upon fish.
Their simple avocation made them gentle, thoughtful,
and kind to each other. In some parts of India, fish
are looked upon as sacred. There is a portion of the

river at Serrinuggur, opposite the Rajah of Cashmere's
Palace, where the largest and heaviest trout are to be
found, upon which no one is allowed to fish, because
the spirits of that monarch's ancestors are supposed,
after death, to have gone into these large trout.
Here, in India, from the native who sits astride of
his chatty, spearing fish as he floats down the Ganges,
to the native Shikari of the Himalayas, who angles
for lordly maseer, or the prawn and pomflet fisherman of Bombay, a strong feeling of unity and
fellow-feeling exists, which is not discernible in others
who, for pastime or a living, engage in other pursuits.

In one word, then, it would seem that the love of
angling, although developing different traits in different
natures, according to temperament, has, in all classes of
mankind and in all nations, a softening, refining, and
romantic influence which no other pursuit of a like
nature can boast of. It is this feeling which, in this
country being developed, enlarged and fostered, has
caused the formation of angling societies and clubs,
whose excellence as institutions, and whose enthusiastic patronage, prove Englishmen to be the first
angling community of the world.

THE FAMOUS WATERLOO RUN OF 1866.

---◆---

IN the good old days of yore, when our forefathers used to make the woodlands of merry England resound with full music from the throats of twenty-five couples of hounds—in those days of which ancient memoir has handed us down the tradition— we learn that foxes were stouter, that men rode harder, and that fences were more impracticable than in the present day. They gloried not in the quick, short, and decisive burst of five-and-twenty minutes, but in the long, dragging, hunting run of three and four hours, where the short-docked, thickset horses were well adapted to keep pace with the throaty, persevering foxhound of that period. Old and grey-headed sportsmen delight to turn round to the youth of the present day with—" Ah ! when I was a boy," &c. Old soldiers are too often apt to exclaim, " The

service is going to the dogs, for when I was a
subaltern," &c.   Old fishermen, too, with a retro-
spective sigh, talk of those "wonderful takes in the
days of yore."   According to the account of these
patriarchs, fox-hunting, shooting, fishing, *et hoc genus
omne*, seem to have been far superior to any the
present epoch can afford.   Now, I should as soon
think of arguing with these worthies as of contra-
dicting a lady; but, nevertheless, facts, as Paley says,
"are stern realities," and the meet of the Pytchley
hounds on February 2nd, 1866, showed that at least
one of the old breed of those stout-going foxes was
still alive, and that the famous Billesdon Coplow run
of former years had at length found its equal.

In endeavouring to describe the incidents of this
never-to-be-forgotten run, I must crave indulgence
wherever I am unable to do full justice to its merits,
and tender an apology to those whose names I may
fail to particularise, it being utterly impossible that
I could be everywhere at the same time.

Friday, the 2nd February, saw Captain Thompson
with his pack of hounds at Arthingworth, situated
three miles from Market Harborough, to the left of
the Northampton road.   This fixture had already
given birth that season to a run which I had described in the columns of *The Field*; and I am free
to assert that the country about Arthingworth,
Clipston, Farndon, and Oxendon is unrivalled by any

that the Pytchley then possessed. The morning broke dull and gloomy, ushered iu with a steady downfall of drizzling rain. There was, however, a certain luminous appearance about the horizon which indicated the probability of its clearing. It being the night of the annual Market Harborough ball, the town was crowded to excess, as also were the various country seats in the neighbourhood. The consequence was that the road to Arthingworth, between half-past ten and eleven, was enlivened by many equestrians and ladies in carriages, all bound to the meet of the Pytchley hounds. In the park, in front of Arthingworth House, were grouped horsemen to the amount of at least two hundred, whilst conspicuous in their centre, some standing, some lying down, were Captain Thompson's own particular pack. These hounds were brought by Captain Thompson with him from Fifeshire into the Pytchley country, and were hunted by him on two days in the week, Dick Roake, the huntsman, officiating with the old Pytchley hounds on the other days.

At twenty minutes past eleven we left Arthingworth for the purpose of drawing Loatland Wood. The day had cleared up, there was a nice soft wind with a dappled grey sky—in fact, all the accessories that make up a really hunting morning. No sooner were the merry pack in covert than a fox was quickly on foot, and, breaking away on the Arthing-

worth side, went straight for Sunderland Wood,
Mr. Fellowes, Captain Robertson, and Mr. Talbot
getting a good start. On his reaching Sunderland
Wood, where Mr. Fellowes arrived as soon as the
hounds, he was unfortunately headed, and, turning
back, retraced his steps to Loatland, the hounds
running a rare pace the whole way. Those who were
left behind in the first start now met the hounds
coming back, and so nicked in. Ten minutes took
them from Loatland Wood to Sunderland Wood, and
nine minutes took them back again. Here Captain
Thompson stuck to him in covert for full a quarter
of an hour, when he was forced out on the Arthingworth side, and eventually ran to ground in a copse,
where some main earths had been carelessly left un-
stopped—an unfortunate circumstance, as the hounds
richly deserved their fox.

Whilst conversing with Mr. Fellowes at the
covertside, he expressed it as his opinion that, from
what he had seen, we were very likely to have a
most extraordinary day's sport; and little did he
think, no doubt, that his prophecy would come so
true. After this we drew Langborough Wood blank,
and from there trotted on to Waterloo Gorse.

And now, my readers, let me endeavour to describe, as far as my poor pen will permit me, one
of the finest runs that has been seen in the shires
for many years, and has never been beaten up to

the present day. The hounds had been but a short
time in covert when a fine fox was viewed away,
pointing for Langborough. A short delay took
place before they got fairly settled to him, which
gave everyone the opportunity of a good start.
When they did, however, go, it was in earnest;
with heads up and sterns down, they skimmed away
over the grass pastures straight into Langborough;
without a pause they press him on through Langborough towards Kelmarsh.

And now let's see who's to the fore. On the
left are Mr. Fellowes, Major Whyte Melville, Mr.
Clarke, Mr. Gosling, and Dick, with Mr. Topham;
while in the immediate wake of the hounds ride
Capt. Thompson, Major Fraser, Mr. J. Chaplin, Capt.
Hoey, Mr. Mills, and some twenty others. Dis-
daining Kelmarsh Covert, he passed in front of
Kelmarsh House, as if he was going for Tally-ho
Gorse, but, altering his mind, he turned sharp to
the right. Leaving Clipston village on our left, we
literally raced over those large pastures in the
neighbourhood of Oxendon and Farndon down to
Lubenham Gorse, the finest line in Northampton-
shire.

The position of the field had now somewhat altered. In the front rank is one who has often been
in the same place on Ascot Heath and Epsom Downs
—Custance, the well-known jockey; with him is Mr.

J. Chaplin, Capt. White, Capt. Hoey, Major Fraser, Mr. Gosling, Mr. F. Langham, the Master, and some ten others.   Of course we thought that the Gorse was his point, but, to our astonishment, leaving it to his left, he crossed the railway and inclined slightly towards Langton; and here your humble servant, with many others, was brought to a standstill, and I am indebted, after using up two horses, for the description of the remaining portion to the Master, who was fortunate enough to be able to get to the end.

After crossing the railway the fox made straight to Great Bowden, crossing the brook, which Custance alone jumped, and into which six unfortunates went; the hounds still running the same pace, and many of the horses in unmistakable trouble, some dying from a gallop to a canter, some ignominiously kicked from a walk into a trot; nevertheless there are some fifteen men still going to hounds.   After crossing the Bowden brook his head is pointed for the finest line in high Leicestershire; leaving Church Langton to his right, on to Gloostone Wood, from which place, leaving Cranhoe to his right he goes at a rattling pace into Keythorpe; and now the select few begin to hope his tale is told, urging on their panting horses to see the last of him.

Curiously enough, the day previous Mr. Tailby had run a fox to ground in Keythorpe Wood, where he had dug him out. Straight for this head of earths

8

did our gallant fox make, but on his arrival, finding that the digging of the day before had upset
the arrangements of his abode, he was forced, the
merry pack being close to him, to press on to save
his brush.

And now many more turned back; Captain Hoey and
Mr. Craven cried a go; Mr. Murietta, Mr. Morrice, and
many others had had enough; indeed, the line the
hounds had come was dotted here and there with men
who were vainly coaxing their wearied horses in a home-
ward direction. Captain Thompson had already ridden
three horses, and was without the aid of either of his
whips or Dick. Never for a moment, however, did the
hounds pause. Leaving Keythorpe Spinneys, they ran
to Hallaton Thorns, from Hallaton Thorns to Fallow
Close; and in the water meadows, Captain Thompson,
Captain White, Mr. Mills, Mr. Chaplin, and Major
Fraser were alone with them. From Fallow Close
they went to Slawston, and eventually the hounds
were whipped off, darkness coming on whilst they
were running in the direction of Medbourn Station.
Major Fraser, Captain White, Mr. J. Chaplin, and
Captain Clarke, with the Master, were, I believe,
the only ones who saw the end of this extraordinary
run.

The time from find to finish was three hours and
forty-five minutes, the distance traversed (not including the back running) from point to point was

eighteen miles, and including the various turns, close
upon six and twenty.

A few more episodes remain to be told. Captain
Thompson, unaided by anyone, took his hounds
home to Brixworth, leaving only two couples behind.
Many of the horses were left at various farmhouses,
being utterly incapacitated from moving any farther.
Doubts seem to be entertained as to our having
changed foxes, but one thing is certain, that as far as
Great Bowden the same fox was in front of the hounds
that left Waterloo Gorse.

Mr. Coventry, who was driving into Harborough,
met the hounds, and putting up his trap at a farmhouse, borrowed a horse from Mr. Angell, at Lubenham, and went with them for a considerable time.
There can be but little doubt that the fastest portion
of the run was from Kelmarsh to Lubenham, which
distance was done in 18½ minutes.

All things, however, must have an end, and no
doubt, had Capt. Thompson been accorded a little more
daylight, this gallant fox would have paid the penalty.
Richly did the hounds deserve him ; so done was he,
that a shepherd dog turned him over two or three
times in a field near Fallow Close. There was
also a great satisfaction for the worthy Master, that
in running through his neighbour's country the
hounds scarcely dwelt a moment in any of the
coverts, nor could they have disturbed any of those

8 *

that Mr. Tailby might intend drawing the next day.

The Harborough ball in the evening was the rendez-vous of the greater portion of those who had been with the hounds in the morning, and the principal topic of conversation, you may be sure, was the famous Waterloo Run of 1866.

THE BIG STAG OF THE GLEN.

---◆---

RED DEER in various portions of the Highlands differ very much in their habits. Those in the forests of Aberdeenshire and Inverness I have always found much easier to get at than those on the Western coasts. The Islands of Mull, Lewis, Harris, Skye, and Jura, all contain red deer, and it is here the stalker meets with something worthy of his steel. Deer-stalking is an art which, like still-hunting in America, is not learnt in a day. It requires patience, endurance, muscles of steel, the power to undergo want, cold, wet, and immense exertion, and then to be ready at the moment your rifle is required, with a steady hand and a quick eye.

The great secret of deer-stalking is to know the lay of the wind, and the man who means to be successful must spare no time or patience to ascertain it. It is

indeed next to impossible to stalk a stag, I mean one
out on the hillside, without having spent at least a
week in studying the ground and learning the wind.
I remember upon one occasion having to go eighteen
miles round for a shot at a stag, and then not getting
within 300 yards of him.   But I know of no moment
that gives the true sportsman such a thrill of pleasure
as the one when, having surmounted all difficulties, he
finds himself within range, with steady nerves pulls the
trigger, and hears the welcome thud of the bullet as it
enters the brown side, stretching the lord of the forest
and glen lifeless on the heather.

As a rule, after the end of August, stags are not
worth shooting except for their heads, for it is now
the rutting season commences and they become thin
and emaciated, but their heads are in splendid condition, not the least vesture of velvet remaining on
their horns.   The best time for deer-stalking, is, in
my humble opinion, the early morning.   I am now
speaking of the Western Highlands.   Deer leave their
beds and feed as soon as the first streak of gray ap-
pears in the east ; they then feed up to seven or eight
o'clock, when they either retire to the woods for shelter, or they lie down in some heathery corrie until the
afternoon, when they again feed until the moon rises.
If in the neighbourhood of turnip fields they will feed
all night, and it is astonishing the amount of injury a
stag and a couple of hinds will do in one night.

Whilst stopping with a friend in Argyleshire some years ago I had the good luck to kill a very old stag that had evaded all efforts, whom the Highland gillies imagined was "no canny"; and as the episode is a good illustration of the difficulties of deer-stalking, I shall endeavour to describe it. The stag had been seen to enter a certain wood the night before, and I felt certain that I should find him somewhere in its neighbourhood in the morning. Accordingly I had made arrangements to be called sometime before sunrise.

A splash of gravel against my window roused me from my bed, and on looking at my watch I found it was half-past four, or about one hour before sunrise. I was soon dressed; a couple of bullets in my sporran, and rifle in hand, I descended the stairs. On the hall-table stood a glass of milk, to which I added a glass of whisky; no bad companion for a November morning. At the hall-door I met the gillie, who was waiting for his "morning," muffled up to his eyes in his plaid. The morning was dark, and a drizzling rain was falling, whilst the fitful moans of the wind, as it passed through the tops of the fir trees, sent a shiver through one, and made you wish yourself back between the sheets.

About a mile from the house there was a loch, the greater portion of which had been drained, leaving a sort of plain about half a mile in extent, covered with coarse grass and straggling clumps of natural birch wood. This basin, as it were, was surrounded by hills, whose heathy sides were dotted here and there with clumps of natural cover, where rank grass and fern grew to a considerable height. At one end of this basin were the remains of the loch, a sheet of water about three acres in extent, whilst traversing the length and breadth ran a small burn. This place was called Loch-nan-Meuhll, or the Loch of the Deer; it was a favourite feeding-ground for those deer who lay in the woods around, and I therefore, naturally, anticipated finding the big stag there.

As we walked along in silence, not a sound was to be heard, except the occasional challenge of some old cock grouse just shaking his feathers to the early morn. Although the dark shadows of the fir trees cast an impenetrable gloom around us, yet on issuing from the woods and striking on to the moor, I found it was far lighter than I anticipated. Quickening our pace, and with the wind in our faces, we soon reached a shepherd's ruined hut immediately over the loch.

The whole basin was wrapt in a heavy mist. There was nothing for it but to crouch under the crumbling wall until the mist should clear away, and the daylight discover the plateau beneath us. Fortunately for us, the few wethers that had been quartered in this part had been removed a few days before, for red deer have the greatest aversion to sheep. I therefore felt almost certain that what deer were in the woods would be out feeding in this their favourite spot.

Anxiously we waited as the gray streaks got broader above the mountain tops, and the mist below wreathed about in fanciful shapes. We could hear the ducks feeding below us, whilst every now and then the sharp warning cry of the curlew broke the silence. Presently the tops of the trees appeared like little islands in a sea of mist, and then one portion, then another, came clearly into view. With my glass glued to my eye, I sought every spot and searched every hollow, but there was nothing to be seen except some old blackcock feeding. Gradually the mist rolled away, settling on the mountain sides, and wreathing round their rocky summits.

At this moment Sandy touched my arm, and pointed to a small gully immediately opposite to us, from which the mist had cleared off. I levelled my glass, and discovered a hind and calf quietly feeding, but no signs of a stag. Again I searched every nook and corner, but to no purpose, and I was just going to get up, light my pipe, and trudge home, when the gillie seized me by the kilt and pulled me down.

"Doun! doun! laird, she's there!" he whispered, whilst every muscle in his face quivered with excitement.

I sank down amongst the wet ferns and heather, and unslung my glass. The gillie carefully pulled a stone

on one side in the ruined wall and pointed to a place
below us.   On covering it with my glass, what was my
astonishment to see a splendid stag about 500 yards
below us, just on the edge of the reclaimed portion of
the loch ; his head was thrown back, and he was sniffing the air, but, alas ! he was to leeward of us, and our
only chance was that, being so much above him, the
taint had not reached him.

The morning was fast advancing, and no time was to
be lost, as deer seek the shelter of the woods very soon,
being disturbed by the farm-labourers and others.
What was to be done ?   A deer-stalker takes in his
position at a glance, and makes up his mind in a
second. I had made up mine. Motioning to the gillie,
I crept into the path leading to the shepherd's hut and
descended into the adjoining valley.   I then turned
down wind and ran about a quarter of a mile until I
reached a small birch wood ; into this I crept.

I was now to windward of the stag, and by the time
I got to the edge of the wood, I was at least a quarter of
a mile below him.   Trembling from head to foot with
the exertion, I unslung my glass and looked up towards
the loch.   He was not there.   Again my eye searched,
until, as I was bringing the glass back to the spot
from whence I had started my survey, I found our
friend.   He had moved, having turned down wind,
and approached nearer to the birch wood in which we
lay concealed.   What was to be done ?   It would not

do to await the chance of his coming within shot, neither could I stir out upon the plain without his seeing me !

My readers will remember the stream I mentioned which flowed out of the loch; this stream had been deepened in order to assist the draining of the loch, and the soil and stones thrown out on either side made a sort of parapet. The stream was about 200 yards distant from the birchwood in which I was kneeling, and not a tuft of grass to conceal me should I venture to cross over it. In a whisper I asked the gillie if the burn could be approached lower down; he said he thought so, and I at once made up my mind what to do.

Giving my glass to Sandy and taking off my sporran, I crawled from tree to tree and from bush to bush, down wind and away from the stag, until I reached the banks of the stream. Breathlessly I dropped into it, and pulled out my flask. Having taken my breath and steadied myself, I commenced ascending the water, and soon arrived at that portion of the stream before described; here it was not necessary to stoop so much, as the banks were higher. As far as I could judge, the stag was about 120 yards from the stream when I last saw him. I had marked a large piece of rock that lay upon the bank as a place about opposite to him, and I now found myself within a few yards of it. Evidently the deer had not moved

or the gillie would have given me notice. My move-
ments were necessarily slow from the cautious manner
in which I was forced to walk in the water, sometimes
up to my ancles and sometimes over my knees; but the
murmur of the stream deadened all sound.

Arrived at the rock I flattened myself against the
the bank, and, gently moving the heather aside, I had
the satisfaction of seeing the stag about fifty yards off,
but moving away from me, and consequently leaving
only his hind quarters to shoot at. In a second my
trusty Rigby rifle was rested on the bank, and I gave a
sharp whistle. The noble animal made a bound forward, and then, turned round and stood stock still.
That moment sealed his fate, as I laid him on the
heather with a bullet through his neck. He was a
very old stag, and very thin, but his head was in perfect
condition and carried ten points. Thus died the "Big
Stag of the Glen." Peace be to his ashes, and may
the same good luck attend my brother sportsmen.

A "SOW JAGD."

WHILST residing at Altenahr in the Rhenish Provinces, I was invited to a "sow jagd," or wild pig shooting. This invitation was in the month of April. Now, as I had never killed a pig in any other way than the legitimate one we have in India—viz. with horse and spear—and knowing the peculiarities of my friends the Germans, so far as anything connected with shooting is concerned, I accepted the invitation not without misgivings as to the safety of my carcass, but promising myself a certain amount of amusement. Accordingly, one chilly morning, I repaired to the rendezvous, which happened to be the village of Honingen on the Ahr. There I found nine or ten jägers assembled, each one having a dog at his heels, and armed with the most extraordinary array of weapons that I ever beheld. As to firing them off, or standing near when such a performance was con-

templated, nothing on earth would have induced me
to do so. Each man had a " jagd-tache," or game-
bag, slung over his shoulders, and, as I said before, a
dog.

Now, I opine it would have troubled the judges of
sporting dogs in *The Field* to have ascertained the
breed of any one of them ; suffice it to say, they were
of all sizes, all shapes, and of various occupations—viz.
from the sheep-dog to the pointer, from the butcher's
dog (for a pair of dogs harnessed to a cart take the
meat from place to place out there) to the kitchen cur.
What on earth a " hühner hund" (*i.e.* a setter or a
pointer) had to do with driving pig, I know not. Each
man had a stick in his hand to help him up the mountain sides, and, of course, his gun slung across his shoulders. They expressed considerable surprise at my having
no sling to my Greener gun, and also asked me for my
jagd-tache or game-bag; but, as I could not possibly
see the use of a game-bag on the present occasion, and
as I far from contemplated the pleasure of carrying a
wild pig on my shoulders, even if I had the luck to
shoot him, I felt perfectly at my ease, although I saw
I had already fallen considerably in their estimations.

When ready for a start, I naturally expected to see
some beaters make their appearance : but no. Off we
trudged to the neighbouring hill, I inwardly deter-
mining to make no remark, but leave the issue to fate ;
though how they expected to shoot pig, unless they

were as thick as rabbits, in this way, I could not imagine. One thing, however, I knew, which was that I should be able to see what game there was in the country, and in what quantity.

After ascending to the top of a very high hill, I, in conjunction with two others, were placed in position, whilst the remainder of the jägers, to the number of seven, were left below to beat up to us with their dogs. Oh! how I waited, and how I cursed, not being able to smoke a pipe.

To make a long story short, the same thing was done in each succeeding range of hills, with a like result; not a " hazel hühn " did I even see, not a hare, not a ghost of a sign even of game.

At length, about 3 P.M. in the afternoon, having climbed up to my allotted position, excessively out of temper, very thirsty, and far from charitably disposed to my neighbours, I was in the act of lighting a pipe to console me in my affliction, when, bang! the report of a gun awoke the echoes around me. "At last," thought I, "but of course he won't come my way, whatever it is." Bang, bang, bang! until the last explosion from my neighbour sent a plentiful supply of buckshot in unpleasant proximity to my person. I believe I said " Hang it!" or perhaps it was something else; but I mentally resolved, if I had been hit, to return the compliment with an Eley's No. 1 wire cartridge of No. 00 that I had in my right barrel. Shouts, yells, and vociferations, now mingled with the yelp, yelp of the curs, told me the game was making in my direction.

Accordingly I stood ready prepared; a movement in the bushes shortly after disclosed a mountain fox quietly sneaking away—of course I did not shoot—when his disappearance was almost immediately followed by two of the noisy curs, the pointer (!) being one of them.

A short time after, my left-hand friend came up to me, accompanied by some of the others, and breathlessly asked me if I had seen him. Of course, thinking he alluded to a pig, I answered "No." "Strange," said he; "the *fox* came straight for you." "Oh! the fox," said I; "oh, yes, I saw him, but I did not think it worth while shooting at him." Tousand, Himmel, Donnery, Wetter, and such like expletives burst from the surrounding jägers, and I still more fell in their estimation. Glad was I to get home, and safely may I say that there is little or no game in that locality—I mean Altenahr. Wild pig do come in the winter-time, and you may get a shot when the snow is on the ground, but it is great labour and very uncertain. There are a few roe deer, partridges, and a very small sprinkling of hares, near Neunahr; but the country is very bare, and no shooting is to be got.

THE PHILOSOPHY OF SHOOTING.

O F all the modern improvements which the sports
man's paraphernalia of to-day presents, none
has made such strides as those of the shot-gun.
As I look back to that ever-memorable birth-day when
I was presented with my first gun, a single barrel with
a rib on it, by James Lang, of Cockspur Street, it is
almost incredible to think what improvements have
been made in gun-making. It is but twenty years
ago I scorned the idea that a breech-loader was as
hard-shooting a gun as a muzzle-loader; and both
in the *Field* and *Land and Water*, I stoutly up-
held the merits of the muzzle-loader as far as hard-
shooting qualities were concerned, though I was faiu to
admit the saving of time and danger through the use of

9

the breech-loader.   Those were the days of the old
" Le Fauchieux " with the awkward underneath lever,
and the pin cartridges with the escapes of gas through
the pin-hole after explosion.   Central fire, hammer-
less, choke-bore guns were not even dreamt of, to say
nothing of concentrators.   Then we shot over dogs,
and never knew what a mantlet meant.   By degrees
bar-locks took the place of back-action locks, then
again rebounding locks, the double-bolted action,
and lastly Mr. Greener's split ejector, an improve-
ment upon Needham's first attempt in that direction;
these, and many others which my space will not allow
me to enumerate, have gone far to improve and perfect
the shot-gun of the present day.   In spite of all
this, the philosophy of shooting remains the same,
and, until man is built in a different mould, it will remain the same to the end of all time, notwithstanding
modern improvements.

There are two important factors common to
human nature which will ever militate against good
shooting; the one is pride, and the other is jealousy.
There is nothing so distressing to a good shot as to
miss frequently comparative easy chances, more especially if the companion he is shooting with, although
by no means so good a shot, does not.   His pride
is aroused, and the harder he tries the wilder he gets,
and the more misses he makes.

I remember once putting this to the test.   I was

shooting with an exceptionally good game shot. Before starting in the morning I arranged with my keeper that the first six cartridges my friend should use should not be loaded with shot. The result was that when he came to the loaded ones he either tailored his birds or missed them altogether. It was useless to explain to him the trick I had played him, and finally he became so nervous that he elected not to shoot any more that day. Jealousy is another feature which is very detrimental to good shooting. In the anxiety to obtain the most shots the sportsman is apt to become excited and to take wild chances; this is always supposing that he is shooting in company. To these two grave faults let me add that when a man who ordinarily shoots well misses, he never pauses to think that his bad shooting is perhaps the consequence of a disordered stomach, or that the business of his every-day life may have been of such a trying nature as to have upset the balance of his nervous system. Again, an uncomfortable hat, an awkwardly-made coat, or a pair of boots that gall or pinch, are more than often conducive to bad and irregular shooting. It is folly to say that a good shot can shoot with any gun; for, inasmuch as no two men are built alike, or walk alike, so is it reasonable to say that the gun which fits one man will not fit another. I have read with considerable amusement the theoretical opinions which have of late been expressed upon the subject of aiming, opinions which

9 *

can and never will be endorsed by practice. The old rule and the golden one, that when the hand and eye go together the object must fall, is infallible.

Shooting, like any other pursuit, such as billiards, cricket, tennis, rackets, &c., depends upon the aptitude of the eye, and it is only when this most sensitive organ of the body is disturbed by other influences that its functions become weakened. Constant practice is another necessity which is involved in successful shooting, especially as to timing. There are certain shots which most men will rarely if ever miss, always providing they are within range; but it is only the professor, cool, calculating and steady, who, no matter how often he misses, or how fewer shots he gets than his companions, will in the aggregate come out at the head of the list.

THE CRUISE OF THE "SPRITE."

NOVEMBER is not exactly the month of the year one would select for a cruise in a 50-ton yawl; and yet the Western Coast of Scotland, with its deep-sea fishing, seal and duck shooting, affords a thousand apologies for choosing a time of the year when the weather is wild and uncertain. Whilst sojourning in the neighbourhood of Tobermory my shooting companion was laid up with a very sharp attack of intermittent fever. His medical attendant, on his recovery, suggested a change of air to remove the debility, and he approved of my idea that a cruise in the "Sprite" might have the desired effect. Now the "Sprite" was a carvel-built boat of 60 feet in length over all, with 15 feet beam, drawing 9 feet 6 inches aft and about 6 feet for'ard. She was strongly built of

oak, her stem and stern posts of American elm, whilst
the midship section of her keel was solid lead, the
ends being American elm.   She was coppered from her
garboard streak up to her water-line with strong copper-
plating and her ballast was half pig-iron, half lead.
She had a full set of sails, including two top-sails, spit-
fire-jib, and trysail, together with a balloon jib and
topsail.   Her standing rigging was of steel, and all her
ropes and running gear of the best white Manilla.
Her accommodation was very good.   The midship
section was, of course, devoted to the saloon, where we
had 7 feet of head-room under the deck; besides this,
there were two cabins aft, and a pantry and cabin forward of the saloon ; the forepart of the vessel being
devoted to the crew, where six hammocks could be
easily swung.   She had a four-oared gig of 18 feet
keel, a dingy, and a duck-boat.   The whole of her fit-
tings on deck were of galvanised iron, and, being perfectly new and copper-fastened throughout, the "Sprite"
with small canvas on her, could make good weather of
it at any time.   Not being built for racing, her spars
and sails were a snug size; and although we have frequently got nine or ten knots out of her with balloon
canvas up and the wind three points free, she was not
a fast boat, but quite enough so for cruising and comfort.   She had a full complement of fishing-gear
consisting of a small trawl, a full set of long lines,
and hand lines, whiffing-lines for mackerel and gurnet;

and a small trammel-net made at Bridport—the most
useful sort of net for a craft to have—completed these
equipments. A crew of three hands and a smart boy
were quite sufficient to work the " Sprite" in any
weather, though we generally took four; and as this
crew was always ready, and could be got from my
friend's estate, we had no sooner matured our plans
than we set about overhauling the " Sprite," getting
in a few stores, and making ready to carry out my
proposed expedition.

There is, perhaps, no coast in the west of Scotland
so much frequented by seals as that of Argyleshire,
especially the islands that lie to the south of the Island
of Skye; and it was with a view to the shooting of
some of these, to have a little cod and ling fishing, and
some duck-shooting, that we were now making our
arrangements. Our crew was soon got together, consisting of old Donald the boatman, his son Angus, and
his nephew Duncan, which with myself, my friend, and
his servant, who acted as steward, made up the crew of
the saucy " Sprite"; the saloon lockers were quickly
filled with bottled beer, soda-water, whisky, rum, tins
of soup, jars of marmalade and jam, tea, sugar, &c.
A sheep was killed, and the carcase, cut up, gracefully
festooned the after-rail of the "Sprite"; the water-
breakers were filled, the coal-bunks supplied, and the
chain locker and anchors overhauled.

Everything was ready within a week, by which time

my friend was so far convalescent as to be able to hobble about with the use of a stick. It was accordingly arranged that we should go on board next day, weigh anchor, and stand over with the flood-tide to Loch Sunart, there being a smaller loch inside it which, we were told, abounded with seals. Next morning, therefore, we embarked in our little craft at low-water. As soon as we were comfortably settled, the mainsail being already set, I gave orders to weigh anchor; we were soon atrip, and, as the anchor came away, we ran up the jib, eased off the mainsheet, and, with a fine breeze from the north-west, stood across for Loch Sunart, some eight miles distant.

As soon as we were fairly under weigh I set the foresail and jigger, and the little craft went staggering along with as much as she could carry. The sounds and lochs on this coast are subject to heavy squalls which come down from the high hills, and require great caution and prudence; but the "Sprite" was as stiff as a church, and stood up under her canvas like a frigate. When, however, we had got into the middle of the sound, not wishing to strain the gear, and being in no particular hurry, I hauled up the main-tack and took the foresail off her, which eased her considerably. It is a very bad plan to carry-on where there is no object, especially if your gear is new, for it gets so stretched that, when you come to anchor, all hands have to turn-to and set up the rigging. Resigning the tiller to Duncan,

I went below to see how my friend fared. 1 found the saloon fire burning brightly, and the cabin warm and snug, and, most fortunately, neither my friend nor his servant suffering from the movement of the vessel.

"I am afraid it is too cold to come on deck," said my friend; "but I should much like to see the entrance to Loch Sunart. It must be very grand."

"Put on your fur coat," said I, "take a rug or a plaid, and you'll be all the better for a good blow on deck."

Just then old Donald put his head down, to tell us that we were abreast of the Stirk Rocks, and consequently in the entrance of Loch Sunart. Accordingly, we went on deck, and as grand a scene broke upon us as we could wish to see. On the right, the Morvin shore stretched away to Artonish, fringed with a snowy wreath of foam; on the left rose the high hills of Ardnamurchan, covered with snow; immediately in front bristled the Stirk Rocks, covered with foam, and thousands of birds screaming about them; whilst the distant hills above Strontian, at the head of the loch, bounded our view.

As we entered the loch the wind shifted to the northward, entailing a pull on the sheets, whilst we stood over for the Ardnamurchan shore. When within half a mile of it I eased the sheets off again and stood down for the point opposite Glenboradaile. We made the

entrance to Loch Teachchush, our anchorage for
that night, a distance of fourteen miles from Tobermory, in less than two hours.

Having come to anchor, had our dinner, and made
everything snug, we began to think what we should do
for the rest of the afternoon. I proposed taking the
gig, and pulling up the loch to see what seals were
there, taking my gun with me for a chance shot
at ducks; accordingly, leaving all on board, I took
Angus with me, and pulled up the loch in search
of sport.

This loch is quite unnavigable, except for small
boats, there being very little water in most parts of it
even at spring-tides; but it is covered with small rocks
which at low tide show themselves in every direction,
and are a favourite resort for seals. Cautiously we
advanced, Angus taking a couple of sculls, whilst I
sat in the bows, my glass in hand, and swept the
loch and shores as we advanced. A low sound from
Angus, and the stopping of the oars, made me turn
round, when I saw two seals right in our wake, about
100 yards distant, looking at us with their large
thoughtful eyes. Bidding Angus crouch down, I
stealthily took up my rifle, whistling a few sharp
notes. The smallest seal immediately advanced some
few yards towards the boat, when I pulled the trigger
and fired; the bullet sped true, and the splash and
commotion told me that I had hit him.

"Pull, Angus," cried I, "pull as if the devil was behind you!" and so he did, being as excited as I was.

When we arrived at the place, the blood and oil on the water showed plainly that I had hit my mark; but although the water was clear, and scarcely three fathoms in depth, we could see no signs of the seal. This is the usual disappointment that the seal shooter encounters with a wounded seal, unless he is fortunate enough to shoot one either on a rock whilst he lies basking, or in shallow water, and he kills him dead. It is next to useless to fire at a seal in deep water, unless you hit him in the head, when he will float for a few moments and give you time, if you are near enough, to get up to him. There is no animal so difficult to approach as a seal, and one or two shots in a place will scare every one in the neighbourhood for the rest of the day. Knowing this, I pulled back to the vessel, somewhat disappointed, killing a couple of Merganser ducks on my way.

As we pulled on board the "Sprite," the evening was closing in, and it was time to set the trammel if we wanted any fish for breakfast. Accordingly I made old Donald hand it down, whilst I stowed it in the stern-sheets of the boat, and, taking him on board, we pulled to some likely-looking ground and set it across the tide.

"Fish is some scarce abut here," said Donald, as we

fastened the last buoy to the net; " but many's the good scringe of herring I've had in this place."

" It looks likely for lobsters, Donald, I think," replied I; " and if we've nothing better to do to-morrow we might shoot one basket of the long lines, and perhaps get conger enough to bait our lobster-pots with."

" It used to be a good enough place," said Donald; " but I'm thinking its well fushed. Hooever, we can try."

As we pulled back to the " Sprite " the last rays of the 'sun sank behind Ardnamurchan, and the chill frosty air made me think of the warm cabin and the hot glass of toddy. On going below, after having seen our anchor-light set on the fore-stay, I found my friend already better for the change and anxious to hear of my adventures, which were soon told over a glass of steaming-hot four-year-old whisky.

We decided upon leaving Loch Teachchush the next morning for some ground round Ardnamurchan point, which Donald told us was the best ground for seals on the coast, intending to look up our old quarters on our return. My friend turned in, and I went on deck to have a look at the weather, see that all was Bristol fashion, and smoke one pipe before turning in.

When I got on deck the wind had dropped to a calm and the clear sky was studded with a thousand stars; the waters of the loch were like a glass mirror, with the huge outlines of the mountains by which it was

surrounded reflected on its surface, deepening the shadows round the shore. All nature was still, the silence
broken only now and then by the wild cry of the guille-
mot, or the shrill challenge of some flock of ducks
as they whistled through the air on the way to the
feeding-grounds. It is such scenes as these that the
loiterer in cities never sees ; it is but to the sportsman whose vagabond propensities lead him to roam
from country to country, and from shore to shore, that
such sights are permitted, where, if he is a man of
thought and intellect, he will find much to reflect
upon.

Let Atheists scoff and unbelievers promulgate their
heathenish doctrines as to the Deity and His divine
attributes. I am prepared to say that they have never
seen God's wonders on the deep, or His works on the
rolling prairies of the west, His terrific magnificence
on the vast summits of the Himalayas or the gorges of
the mighty Cordilleras, or where the hurricane with all
its horrors sweeps devastation and destruction over the
islands of the Southern seas; or, bound up with the
mighty cords of frost, His power is shown in the
northern latitudes amongst seas of ice. I have seen
them all, and worship the Hand that decreed them, and
that Almighty protection that permits man to view
the vast works of his Maker and learn what an insignificant unit he is in so vast a creation.

The day was just breaking when, sailor-like, I turned

out of my bunk; a jerk at my cabin-bell and a "morning," pulled me together, and I found my way up to the slippery deck.

"Rig out the gangway, Donald, and get the boat alongside; we'll take up the trammel," I said, "whilst Angus and Duncan wash the deck down."

The boat was hauled alongside, and off we set to see what luck we had for our breakfast.

The net was soon hauled aboard, with but little inside it. There were a few cuddies, a small cod, a silver haddock—enough, however for a fry; with these we returned to the "Sprite," and I soon heard them hissing and spluttering over the stove. Meantime I roused up my friend, and then went into my cabin to perform my toilet. Breakfast over—and one that can alone be eaten with an appetite procured by such pursuits as ours—I went on deck to get under weigh. The covers were soon off the sails, the mainsail set, and the windlass-handles at work. Meantime the weather had changed, the sky was becoming overcast, and thick banks of clouds were gathering in the westward; the glass too had fallen considerably, and every indication of a smart breeze of wind warned me to make all snug. Accordingly, I shifted the large jib, took a reef in the foresail, and one in the mainsail, housed the top-mast, and had the boats swung inboard and lashed. I then got up the tarpaulins to cover the hatches, served out a glass of grog all round, got the

anchor up to the bows, and, with the wind one point
on the starboard bow, we left Loch Teachchush.

"Cot, sir! I'm thinking we'll hae a gude thrashin'
at it afore we get round the Rhue; and there's nay
anchorage, unless ye run back home," said Donald, as
he came aft to where I stood steering the vessel.

"We can hold on in Queenish Bay, on the one side,"
answered I, "or Mingary on the other, Donald; but
we won't insult the 'Sprite' by putting back without a
try."

"Weel, weel, laird, it's a gude bit boat, and she kens
her ainsel as weel as I do what we are likely to get off
the point."

"Stand by, for'ard," I cried, "ready about! helm's
a-lee, jib-sheet!" and round spun the "Sprite" on her
heel like a top. "Let draw and belay!" and she was
speeding on on the other tack, looking well up for the
Stirks.

As we drew out from the shelter of the Ardnamurchan
shore the wind increased and the sea began to get heavy.
I was compelled, therefore, to take another reef in the
mainsail and dispense with the foresail altogether, and
under this small canvas storm-jib and double-reefed
mainsail we made the Stirks.   Once more we went
about, and, the wind being now on the beam, the
sheets were eased off, and we stood for Ardnamurchan
point.

A few small flakes of snow began to fall, and I

almost felt inclined to make for home; but then, again, it was a dead nose-ender, and if the worst came to the worst, we had but to turn back and run for our old anchorage. We were making some five knots through the water, when, looking up to windward, a sight caught my eye that made me wish I had not left my anchorage. About a mile distant the sky looked like one bank of lead, and a wall of foam and mist was rapidly advancing. I knew what it meant, and prepared to meet it.

"Stand by the jib-sheet; flat it well in, lads!" I cried. "Donald, take the helm, and keep her 'full and by,' a hand aft to the main sheet, and rouse it in! steady, so; belay; keep good way on her, Donald, and don't go any higher."

"Ay, ay, Sir!" cried the old seaman, as he crammed his Sou'wester down, and took a fresh quid.

Those of my readers who know anything about seamanship will easily understand that by these manœuvres I had got the "Sprite" close-hauled on the port tack, standing as close to the wind as I dared, without her sails shaking. She was thus looking up to the shore of the island with Ardnamurchan point on our beam. Scarcely had these arrangements been made when the snow-storm burst upon us with all its fury; the air was filled with snow, and you could see nothing beyond the bowsprit end. The "Sprite," however, behaved well, rising like a duck to the seas, and standing stiffly up under her double-reefed mainsail and storm jib.

It is a curious circumstance, but there is, perhaps, nothing that affects the compass so much as a snow-storm. In the present instance the card fairly traversed all round, so that, had we been out of sight of land, we should have had to have taken an observation to find our whereabouts, on the first opportunity.

Whilst I was looking at the binnacle, a sudden crash aloft made me start, thinking we had carried away our mast; but it proved to be the strop of the throat-halliard block that had given way, and let the luff of the sail down. Immediately I ordered the foresail to be run up, the peak halliards let go, and the jigger set, and under this canvas the "Sprite" went to windward in gallant style.

Here is a wrinkle worth knowing, and of which a practical illustration has just been given. When getting under weigh, it is always well to have a strop of stout rope passed round the mast and one end made fast to the jaws of the gaff, the other end to the crosstrees; so that, in case any such accident should happen as the one just described, the sail is supported by the strop, and does not come down on deck.

The snow-storm soon cleared off, and, having repaired our damages, we eased the sheets off and ran for Mingary, which bay we reached in the afternoon, coming to anchor in seven fathoms of water.

Towards evening the strong breeze had blown itself out, and as I deemed our anchorage somewhat too open and exposed, should the wind shift to the southward, I weighed anchor, set the foresail, and stood in to Killundrie Bay, coming to anchor abreast the clergyman's house. As soon as everything had been made snug I pulled ashore to see if I could procure any bait in the village for our long lines, whilst Donald went off to set the trammel. I was fortunate enough to obtain four large conger-eels, and some fresh herring, enough to bait five hundred hooks. With this I returned on board, and after supper the crew turned to, to bait the lines.

A long line, or as it is called in England a "trot," and in Ireland a "spiller," is of very simple construction, and is generally used in deep water for cod, ling, halibut, turbot, scate, and conger, smaller lines on the same principle being used for flounders, whiting, and codlings.

The lines we had were dressed with large hooks for cod and ling, each tray or basket containing about 200 hooks, with a fathom distance between each hook—the length of the foot-line being 250 fathoms, and the buoy-lines 40 fathoms each. The best bait for the large lines are buckies or whelks, fresh herring and conger. Halibut is also an excellent bait.

When fishing with small lines, mussels, and lugworm, with bits of crab, are excellent, especially the small soft crab found in the fissures of the rocks. These are an almost irresistible attraction to flounders and whiting.

The best time to shoot long lines is at about half-tide, and to let them fish for two hours; but the line can be run over, and those hooks that are found to be unbaited can be rebaited, what fish are on it taken off, and the line left for any length of time, if the ground is good, and there are many fish about. Some fishermen shoot them in the evening, and take them up at sunrise, letting them fish all night; but I do not think this is a good plan, as if there are many large fish on the line, they are sure to get it foul, and in many cases get off.

The next morning after breakfast, the tide being suitable, we put 500 hooks into the gig, and pulled out to a bank between the mainland and the island about four miles distant from our anchorage. The line is very easily shot, but care must be taken in paying it out to prevent the hooks fouling one another, as in such a case the whole tray or basket would be in a tangle.

The man who shoots the line stands in the stern sheets, whilst the men at the oars paddle gently. The buoy-line with the stone attached is first hove overboard to leeward, and the men rest on their oars until the stone touches the bottom. As soon as this happens the boat is pulled gently ahead, and the foot-line

10 *

is paid out over the leeward side of the boat until the end is reached, when the boat stops, and the other buoy-line is attached, and the stone sunk to the bottom. The buoys are generally made of inflated dog or sheep skins, and the advantage of having two buoys is, that in case one gives way, there is always the other to mark the end of the line.

We shot our line in 35 fathoms of water, and then pulled in towards Queenish Bay to fish with hand-lines until it was time to take up the "trot." We let go our anchor in 15 fathoms, and with lug for bait, we were soon hard at work, but with little success. We caught a few codlings, and a whiting or two, but the cuddies annoyed us very much by taking our baits off continually. However, by dint of a smoke, and stories from Donald about seals, which only whetted our appetites to be at them, we managed to pass away the time. At length it was time to return, and see what monsters we had caught, and with a dram to cheer us and "for luck," we pulled off to the lines.

Now shooting a long line is comparatively easy work, but the hauling that long line up is a very different thing altogether. In the first place your fingers get dreadfully cold, and if there are heavy fish they pull so hard that your back and loins ache after you have got but a few fathoms aboard, and in a heavy sea it requires great care not to be pitched overboard. A short gaff is indispensable to hook the fish into the boat, and a short stout club to hit them over the head, and prevent them from splashing about.

Having reached the nearest buoy I hauled it aboard, coiling the buoy-line up until I got to the stone. I then took it off, and commenced with the foot-line, coiling it away into one of the trays. The first few hooks produced nothing, and I began to think our labour had been in vain, when a jerk or two at the line told me there was a fish near.

I forgot to say that the line was shot *across* the tide, and that in taking it up the person who does so stands in the stern sheets, and the boat is backed as the line comes in.

"Easy, lads, here 's a good one !" I cried, as a large cod of about 20 pounds came floundering to the surface, and Donald who had the stroke oar, hooked him in with a gaff.

"Come, Sir, that 's better than nothing," said he.

"Look out for another. Halloa ! what on earth 's this? it looks like a hip-bath got foul of one of the hooks," said I.

"Hech ! hech ! did ever a body see a scate like that !" said Duncan, as an enormous fish of that species came to the surface. "He 's over big for the boat, Sir; cut him away, and let him go adrift."

"Hoot tout, Sir, dinna do the like at all, he 'll be grand bait, just go fair and canny. So, ye great ugly

beast," said Donald, as, after frightful exertion and
many slips, he managed to get him into the boat. I
roared with laughter at the struggle between the fish
and Donald until my sides ached. And so we went on
until we had taken 23 cod and ling, 3 scate, and 4
congers. Before half the time was up, however, I was
dead beat, and forced to hand over the rest to Donald,
while I took to the gaff; infinitely less labour, and
quite as amusing.

We then pulled back to the "Sprite," arriving
about 3 o'clock in time for dinner, and giving us the
rest of the evening to make preparations for our start
for Seal Island, as I shall call it, next morning.

Before I proceed with our adventures on board the
"Sprite," it would be as well to say something about
seals, and the species that are found upon the west
coast, together with their habits and distinctive
marks.

The west coast furnishes three distinct species.
Two of these species I have shot, and the third I have
seen, although I have never been able to procure a
specimen. The common seal (*Phoca Vitulina*) or, as
it is called by the Highlander, "Rawn"; the grey seal
(*Phoca*) called in Gaelic "Tapvaist"; and the small
seal, the Latin name for which I am unable to discover—the Highlanders, however, call them "Bodach,"
or the Old Man.

The usual length of the "Rawn," or common seal,

seems to be about 5 feet to 5 feet 6 inches from the nose to the end of the extremities. They are found in considerable quantities on the western coast, and frequent sounds and flats where fish is abundant, and the water not very deep. Their favourite food seems to be flounders, probably because being a flat fish they are easily caught. They do not, however, confine themselves particularly to this sort, as I have see them at the mouths of salmon rivers, especially at the mouth of the "Shiels," where I have no doubt salmon often varied their bill of fare. I have seen them even as high up as the brackish water, but never in fresh. They breed about the month of June, and the female produces sometimes one and sometimes two calves. They are usually whelped in some deep cavern, and shortly after their birth they go to sea. The weight of the adult varies very much, but I have shot one of 14 stone. The colour is a dark tawny white, covered over the back and sides with brownish black spots ; the paws and fins, or feet, are of a darker colour, and the belly dusky grey ; the skin, if I may so call it, is wholly destitue of fur, but is covered with short, thick-set hair, strong and hard to the touch.

The grey seal, or " Tapvaist," is a larger animal than the common seal, and does not occur so frequently on the shores of the mainland, although I have seen them very often on the west coast of Skye,

North and South Uist, and about Barra Head. The
uniform colour is a sort of silvery grey, besprinkled
with black splotches. From a peculiarity in the hair
of the adult, the hair being considerably recurved, the
animal when dry, and with its hair turned towards one,
seems a sort of silvery grey, especially if the sun is
shining upon it, but if looked at in an opposite direction the appearance of the colour becomes at once a
sort of dirty brown ; the muzzle of a blackish colour,
and the eyes large and round.

The "Bodach," or Old Man, is much the same in
shape, colour, and habits, as the common seal, but is
neither so large, nor so shy in its habits. There is,
however, a curious formation in connection with the
structure of the eye in this animal that is worthy
of notice. At the inner angle of the eye will be
found a third eyelid, which can be easily drawn over
the whole of the eye, and seems to have been placed
there as a protection against external dangers of any
kind.

From carefully watching the habits of these animals
I find that they seem excessively fond of going on
shore frequently, especially on hot, sunny, summer
days, and they generally do this every tide. They
select the flattest and most shelving rocks that have
been covered at high water, and are separated from
the mainland. The time they generally choose is half-
ebb, and when they stretch themselves upon a rock

they generally lie with their heads off shore, and as close to the water as possible. They have a keen scent, and can wind anyone approaching to a considerable distance. When in large numbers together, they generally place one of their number, as it were on sentry, who gives notice of any danger. They always seem to prefer small rocks—for the reason, I conclude, that they are less easily approached. They remain on shore from three to four hours, till the rise of the tide compels them to seek other ground. A seal is easily tamed, and they become great pets. No greater proof of this is to be seen than that of the seal now in possession of the Zoological Society in Regent's Park, where he leaves the water at the call of the keeper, and follows him wherever he goes—standing up against the iron rails of his pond, and pressing his muzzle against his cheek.

Several instances of tame seals have also occurred in the Highlands, where they have been caught when young, and have lived in the cabins, going every now and then to the sea.

Extraordinary to say, also, they seem particularly partial to lying as close to the fire as possible, and when they have been removed invariably wriggling themselves back to the heat.

Upon reference to other authors upon the natural history of the seal, we find that they have at one time been used as articles of food. Sir R. Sibbald tells us

that the people in the Island of Uist attack the seals and
kill them, selling the skins, but salting the carcases,
which they eat in time of Lent as sweetly as venison.
Another author* states that in North Ronaldsay they
were captured for the purpose of eating, and were said
to make good hams.

According to Dean Monroe,† the seals of Islay were
slain by the help of trained dogs ; and another author
informs us that seals were slaughtered by the inhabitants in the following manner. They watched the
seals lying upon certain rocks, and when the tide was
fairly ebbed they placed themselves at the only out-
lets, and then created a disturbance, so as to move the
seals, and as they endeavoured to escape stunned them
with clubs, and then despatched them. This system is
still pursued by the proprietor of the Island of Canna,
where, at a certain time every year, many seals are
slaughtered with clubs. Again, Mr. Edmonston informs us that they have been caught in Shetland in
nets, but I have also heard of the same method having
been used on the west coast farther south. Seals, we
are told, were known to the ancient Romans, who considered that their skins were a protection against
lightning. They used to make huts, and cover them
with their hides.

The seal that is found on the western coast must

---

* Low.   † Martin's Western Islands.

not, however, be confounded with that valuable animal the "Fur seal" (*Otaria Falklandica*); the skin of the seals I have been endeavouring to describe being of too coarse a texture to admit of its being used for ladies' cloaks, muffs, or tippets. It is, however, often made into coats, and very comfortable they are.

At the outset of these remarks I should have stated that naturalists of the present day have divided the seal tribe into two great species, the first one called the Inauriculata, or earless seals, and second, the Otaries, or eared seals. The peculiar characters of the Phocae proper are, that their feet are enveloped in the integuments, so becoming swimming paws; the anterior are very short, and the posterior much in the same line with the body; they have no external ears, and the toes of the feet are webbed and terminated by sharp claws.* With regard to the other species, the Otaries, as they are the inhabitants of another clime, I do not consider it my province to describe them in these pages, the more so, as I am not acquainted with them except from the perusal of books on natural history. Having therefore, I trust, interested my readers, to a certain extent, in connection with the seal, I shall proceed with our adventures on board the "Sprite" in search of them.

The next morning, the day being fine and the wind

---

* Sir William Jardine, Bart.

fair, we set sail for the island that Donald had told us of, and which lay to the south-east of the Island of Canna. After a fair run of three hours, we came to anchor off the Island of Musk, and sat down to breakfast. Cod-steaks nicely broiled, a bit of turbot curried, and some fried ham and eggs, are no bad things after a three hours' blow on the stormy Atlantic.

I need hardly say we did full justice to our fare; and when, after satisfying the inner man, we buttoned ourselves up in warm pea-jackets, and went on deck to smoke the post-prandial pipe, with the blue sea around us, the hills on the mainland rising boldly up in the distance, whilst the Scour of the Island of Eig shot up into the blue vault on our starboard bow, and the waters danced merrily in the sunshine, I fancied myself at peace with all mankind, and the happiest fellow alive.

Donald thought that we should make the Island of Canna that evening, it being only twenty-five miles distant, and the wind and tide with us; therefore, as soon as the men had breakfasted, we hove short, made sail, and kept her away north by east, leaving the Island of Eig on our starboard hand, and steering for the southernmost part of the Island of Rum. Soon the lofty peak of Benmore was distinctly seen, crowned with mist, and as we kept away half a point to the eastward, we opened the Island of Canna, which place we reached about 3 P.M. after a rattling run of three hours and a quarter.

We came to anchor under the laird's house, and having landed and asked for leave to wage war against the seals, we obtained his kind permission, and returned on board to dinner, though his Scotch hospitality would fain have detained us; but so anxious were we to commence operations, that we excused ourselves in the best way we could, and returned on board.

Whilst at anchor, several seals showed themselves in our neighbourhood, and it was with difficulty that I restrained my friend from having a shot. Whether he slept that night or not, I am not prepared to say; but, on my turning out at break of day, I found him both up and dressed, and giving his rifle a rub over.

" My dear fellow," said I, " you are full two hours too early; it is of no use going over to the island until dead low-water, and the tide has only ebbed three hours."

" Well, you see," he replied, " I couldn't sleep, and I've been laid up so long that, somehow or another, my activity seems to have taken a fresh lease, and I'm fit for anything. You see, it will take us about an hour to get ready and pull over to the island, so that we've just got an hour to spare; so if you'll give William a hail, in order that we may have something for breakfast, I'll see the traps stowed in the boat."

Our arrangements were soon completed, the boat loaded, and all in order by the time that breakfast was announced; that meal was soon despatched, and about an hour and a half before low-water we started for our ground, having previously made the stern determination not to fire a shot, no matter how tempting, until we had arrived at our ground.

The weather was all that could be desired at that season of the year; the sea calm, and the sun shone bright after a hard frost in the morning, and everything was bathed in sunshine as we left the side of the "Sprite." After a good hour's pull, we got under the lee of our island, and a truly desolate "sealy" place it looked. The rocks, like all those of the islands of the western coast, seemed heaped upon one another in the most disorganized way, as if some violent eruption had tossed them into the air, and they had remained , as they fell for years and years. It is a thing to be remarked, that in all the islands of the Hebrides, there are no primary symptoms to be seen in their geological formations.

As we drew near the island, we exercised the greatest caution for fear of disturbing the seals at their siesta, and I narrowly examined the place without being able to understand Donald's method of proceeding.

To all appearances it seemed nothing but a rock about a mile in circumference, rising abruptly from the water,

its sides indented with hollows or caves, formed by
the constant churning and fretting of the Atlantic,
and without a sign of vegetation upon it. Immediately
opposite to us, however, there appeared a sort of small
sandy cove, scarce large enough to admit of our
boat, towards which we were approaching with great
caution, the wind being in our teeth.

As the nose of the boat grated noiselessly on the
sand, we landed cautiously and quickly, one by one,
when we found ourselves upon a small platform, as it
were, of sand, and a scarped rock surrounding us on
all sides, apparently inaccessible. Donald, however,
pointed out to us a sort of stair cut in the rock, up
which we crept, and, having reached a fissure a con-
derable height up, he desired us to look through, and,
as I was the first, I did so, and was fairly taken aback
by the scene.

The centre of the rock seemed to me like a cauldron,
which was filled from the ocean through a passage
about twelve feet in breadth, exactly opposite to
us. This salt-water lake, if I may so call it, was
now nearly dry, and upon the small pieces of weed-
covered rock that dotted its surface basked several
seals.

After looking at this strange freak of nature for
some little time, caused doubtless by a volcanic
eruption of bygone days, I turned my attention to
the seals. There were, as far as I could see, about

a dozen, some asleep, others lazily stretched on the
rocks, whilst one or two were chasing one another
in the water, the depth of which could not at the
utmost have been more than three feet.

Our dispositions were soon made. My friend and
I were to gain the opening opposite by creeping round
the rocks, and as Donald frightened the seals we
were to shoot as they made out through it for the
open sea. I bargained, however, for a shot at an old
bull seal that lay on a rock by himself, monarch of all
he surveyed, and I begged Donald not to show himself
until I had fired. My friend went to the right, I
crept to the left, and after half-an-hour's crawling
and creeping, I found myself in the right spot. My
friend had, however, not yet arrived, and I waited in
the greatest fear that the seals would wind me, and
commence making off. I took stock of the old bull
seal, who still lay in the same position, and, as far as
I could judge, about 100 yards off.

He seemed to be a little uneasy, fidgeting
about and sniffing the air. I was, however, a little
out of his line, but I suspect that he winded my
friend, and, accordingly, I rested my rifle over a rock
in front, and prepared to fire. My rifle was a poly-
groove one, No. 12 bore, a muzzle-loader, made by
Rigby, and sighted up to 200 yards. I put up the
100-yards sight and drew bead, with my finger on
the trigger. At that moment my friend gave a low

whistle; I touched the trigger, the bullet sped true, and with a thud entered the seal's body.

The report woke up ten thousand echoes, whilst, with such a splashing and commotion as I never saw, the seals made for our opening in order to get to sea, and, as one came up, my friend let drive, but missed, when they all turned back, diving again, and in the clear shallow water we could see them darting about like huge fish. Meantime my seal rolled into the water, dyeing the surface with blood and oil, and lashing about in a furious manner; but his struggles were soon over, and I saw his carcase lying inanimate, half submerged. Meantime, the seals occasionally put up their heads, when my friend's rifle cracked again and again, but to no purpose.

At last I motioned to him not to fire any more, but to conceal himself, in the hope of inducing the seals to make for the opening into the sea, when we could get a shot with a certainty as they wriggled their bodies over the ledge of rock that closed the opening to the lake, but thirty yards distant from our position. We lay perfectly still for full half an hour, and I began to get impatient.

Upon looking at the rock, I saw the tide was making rapidly, when, of course, the seals would be able to escape through the opening under water. The only chance to get another, and secure the one I had shot, therefore, was to risk a shot at the head of one

11

as he came up for breath. Cautiously peeping over,
I saw a head, about fifty yards off, evidently recon-
noitring the opening.   I accordingly determined to
venture a shot.   I pulled the trigger, aiming about
half-an-inch under his head ; the bullet was true, and
hit fair; the seal, instead of diving, commenced
whirling round and round on the surface of the water,
and in a few minutes disappeared.

I then shouted to Donald that the tide was making,
and that we had better secure our booty, as the water
was already coming over the ledge of rock that
closed the entrance.   The last seal I had shot was
found quite dead at the bottom, and, having secured
the other, we dragged them off in triumph to the boat.
As we were leaving we could see the seals making off
through the opening, upon which there must have
been by this time quite two feet of water.

Donald told us that the way the people killed them
was by going once or twice a year, in a party of twenty
or thirty, leaving four men with clubs to guard the
entrance.   The others then went into the water, and
drove the seals to the opening, where they were
stunned by the clubs of those stationed there.   The
old bull seal I had killed was a grand fellow, five
feet five inches in length, measuring from the extremities; whilst the other was apparently a young one,
measuring about four feet six inches.

After thus disturbing their retreat, it was evident

we should have no more chance, as the seals would not return for perhaps another three weeks, at least, Donald said so. After, therefore, having a day at the ducks round the island, we determined upon running up the Sound of Islay, in the hope of finding another seal preserve; but with the exception of one bodach that my friend killed with B.B., we had no luck, although we fired a good many shots.

We had now been absent three weeks, during which time my friend had thoroughly recovered; and what with some excellent duck-shooting and deep-sea fishing, together with our three seals, we had no insignificant bag to boast of on our return to Tobermory, for which place we set sail, dropping our anchor, after a twenty-four hours' passage from the Sound of Skye, in the bay of that name.

LONDON :

PRINTED BY W. H. ALLEN AND CO., 13 WATERLOO PLACE, S.W.

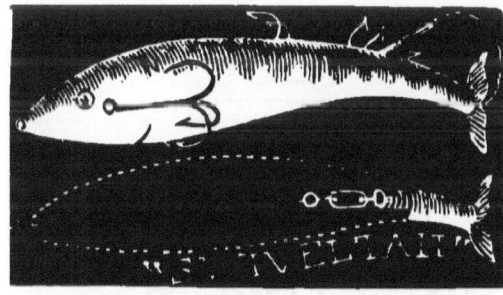

BOOKS ON HORSES AND RIDING.

New and Cheaper Edition. 8vo., half-bound, 10s. 6d.

ILLUSTRATED HORSE DOCTOR. Being an Accurate and De- tailed Account, accompanied by more than 400 Pictorial Representations, characteristic of the various Diseases to which the Equine Race are subjected; together with the latest Mode of Treatment, and all the requisite Prescriptions written in Plain English. By EDWARD MAYHEW, M.R.C.V.S.

New and Cheaper Edition. 8vo., 7s. 6d.

ILLUSTRATED HORSE MANAGEMENT. Contains Descriptive remarks upon Anatomy, Medicine, Shoeing, Teeth, Food, Vices, Stables; likewise a plain account of the situation, nature, and value of the various points; together with comments on grooms, dealers, breeders, breakers, and trainers; Embellished with more than 400 engravings from original designs made expressly for this work. By E. MAYHEW. A new Edition, revised and improved by J. I. LUPTON, M.R.C.V.S. Crown 8vo., Illustrated, 6s.

THE MANAGEMENT AND TREATMENT OF THE HORSE, IN THE STABLE, FIELD, AND ON THE ROAD. By WILLIAM PROCTER (Stud Groom). Second Edition, revised and enlarged.

" There are few who are interested in horses will fail to profit by one portion or another of this useful work."—*Scotsman.*

"We cannot do better than wish that Mr. Procter's book may find its way into the hands of all those concerned in the management of the most useful quadruped we possess."—*England.*

"There is a fund of sound common-sense views in this work which will be interesting to many owners."—*Field.*

"Coming from a practical hand, the work should recommend itself to the public."—*Sportsman.*

Crown 8vo., with Portrait, 5s.

LADIES ON HORSEBACK; Learning, Park-Riding, and Hunting. With Hints upon Costume, and Numerous Anecdotes. By Mrs. POWER O'DONOGHUE (Nannie Lambert), Authoress of " The Knave of Clubs," " Horses and Horsemen," &c.

"Thoroughly practical, dealing with learning, park-riding, hunting, and costumes, and written in a style that is sure to win readers. We heartily recommend the book." —*Graphic.*

"A very complete and useful manual, written in a pleasant, lady-like way by a thorough mistress of the subject, and full of valuable hints."—*Vanity Fair.*

"Mrs. Power O'Donoghue has laid that large and increasing number of her sex devoted to equitation under a deep debt of gratitude by the production of this charming volume."—*Irish Sportsman.*

Crown 8vo., price 2s. 6d.

HOW TO RIDE AND SCHOOL A HORSE. By E. L. ANDERSON.

"It requires the study of only a very few pages of this book to convince the reader that the author thoroughly understands his subject."—*Illustrated Sporting and Dramatic News.*

"Concise, practical directions for riding and training, by which the pupil may become his own master."—*Land and Water.*

Crown 8vo , 2s. 6d.

A SYSTEM OF SCHOOL TRAINING FOR HORSES. By E. L. ANDERSON, Author of " How to Ride and School a Horse."

"He is well worthy of a hearing."—*Bell's Life.*

"Mr. Anderson is without doubt a thorough horseman."—*The Field.*

London : **W. H. ALLEN & Co., 13 Waterloo-place.**

TOMLINSON'S
IMPERIAL

HORSES   CATTLE

SHEEP   DOGS

EMBROCATION.

Chapped Heels.	Sore Shoulders.
Broken Knees.	Capped Hocks.
Sore Throats.	Rheumatism.
Wind Galls.	Sore Backs.
Over-reaches.	Influenza.
Strains.	Bruises.
Sprains.	Wounds.
Splints.	Curbs.

Sore Mouths in Sheep and Lambs.
Foot Rot in Sheep.
Sprains, Cuts, and Bruises in all Animals.

Price 2/- per bottle.

May be had from

Messrs. BARCLAY & SONS, 95, Farringdon Street,

Of all Chemists, or post free of the Maker, at

9, Langton Street, Chelsea.

12

GEORGE CURRELL,

Fly & Fishing Tackle Maker,

64, Parchment Street,

WINCHESTER.

The above has purchased Mrs. Cox's well-known business, and is ready to supply all the best Patterns of

TROUT AND GRAYLING FLIES.

TO LET.

Two Miles of the best water on the Itchen below Winchester, by Season Ticket.

Highly recommended by "Light Cast" and the late Mr. Francis Francis.

SPRATTS PATENT

Meat "Fibrine" Vegetable

DOG CAKES

(WITH BEETROOT).

Beware of Worthless Imitations!

SEE EACH CAKE IS STAMPED

SPRATTS PATENT AND A "X."

Cod Liver Oil Dog Cakes,

FOR PUPPIES AFTER DISTEMPER, AND FOR DAINTY FEEDERS AND SICK OR PET DOGS.

DISTEMPER POWDERS, WORM POWDERS, MANGE, ECZEMA, AND EAR CANKER LOTIONS, TONIC CONDITION PILLS, &c.

PAMPHLET ON CANINE DISEASES, AND FULL LIST OF MEDICINES, POST FREE.

POULTRY MEAL,

The most Nutritious and Digestible Food for Chicks and Laying Hens (being thoroughly cooked). Samples Post Free

---

New Edition of "THE COMMON SENSE OF POULTRY KEEPING," 3D., POST FREE.

"Spratts Patent Limited," London, S.E

FISHING GUT.

....

The only Gold Medal for best General Gut Exhibit, International Fisheries Exhibition, London, 1883, was awarded to

ROBERT RAMSBOTTOM,

GUT IMPORTER AND
FISHING TACKLE MANUFACTURER,

81, Market Street,

MANCHESTER.

....

The Gut Report and Price List for Current Year will be forwarded ˉon receipt of addressed envelope.

JOHN RIGBY & CO.,

GUN AND RIFLE MAKERS

By Appointment to H.R.H. Prince of Wales.

ESTABLISHED 1760.

PATENTEES OF VARIOUS IMPROVEMENTS IN

Hammerless Guns and Rifles,

ALSO OF

A NEW EJECTOR GUN.

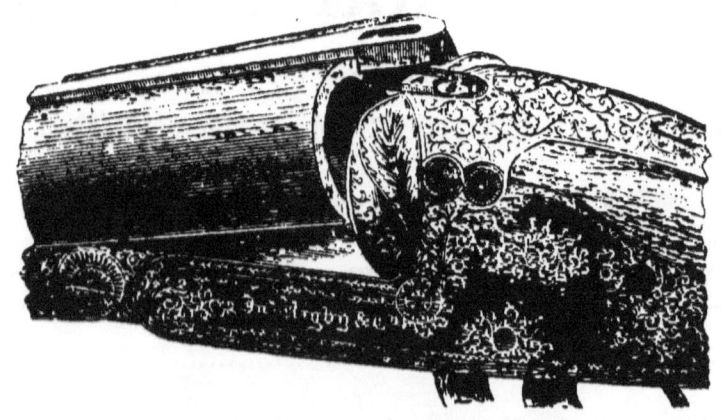

Price Lists on application to

72, ST. JAMES'S STREET, LONDON;

and 24, SUFFOLK STREET, DUBLIN.

GOLD MEDAL
GUNS AND RIFLES.

Strongest actions made, suitable alike for Large Bore Rifles or Small Bore Guns.

Perfect Safety; cannot be snapped off when the barrels are removed from the action.

ONLY HIGH-CLASS PRACTICAL WORKMEN EMPLOYED.

Testimonials.

AN OFFICER writes: "Upper Burmah, Nov. 16, 1886.—I have used the Rifle a good deal, and find it matchless for accuracy. I am delighted with it in every way.—E. R. P."

ANOTHER OFFICER writes: "India, July 13, 1887.—The Gun and Rifle I got from you were first-class. Later on I shall want an 8-bore Rifle and a good Rook Rifle.—Capt. A. A. P."

ANOTHER LETTER, received July 9, 1887: "The ·500.Bore Express Rifle you supplied I have shot with a good deal, and I find it everything I could wish."

GUNS.

Highest Quality, with or without Hammers	45 Guineas.
Same Quality as above, Plainer Finish	40 ,,
Second Quality	30 ,,
,, Plainer Finish	25 ,,

We have also Machine-made Guns, from £10 to £18.

RIFLES.

Highest Quality, any calibre	55 Guineas.
Second ,, ,, ...	40 ,,
Plain ,, ,, ...	25 ,,

CARTRIDGES at Store Prices.

In Cartridges loaded by J. L. & SON, the best quality Powder, Shots, Wads, and Cases are used only (guaranteed).

Only Address: 22, COCKSPUR ST., PALL MALL.